Frank pop d set it to Play. "Le e said to Joe.

For a moment there was static, then a picture appeared with no sound. On the screen it was winter. Two men—one old, one young—both wearing army uniforms stood on the steps before a large white house.

"Those are Russian uniforms!" Joe exclaimed.

Frank nodded. "The older man's a colonel."

On the screen the two men were arguing now. The younger man's face became an expressionless mask as he raised a gun. The older man fell backward down the steps of the building, his blood staining the snow.

Joe's eyes widened. "Frank—that soldier . . ."

Frank nodded, his mouth suddenly dry. The face on the screen, the man who had shot the older officer—

It was their brother, Chris.

Books in THE HARDY BOYS CASEFILES® Series

Available from ARCHWAY Paperbacks

THE HARDY BOYS CASEFILES NO. 22

DOUBLE EXPOSURE

FRANKLIN W. DIXON

AN ARCHWAY PAPERBACK
Published by POCKET BOOKS
New York   London   Toronto   Sydney   Tokyo

AN ARCHWAY PAPERBACK *Original*

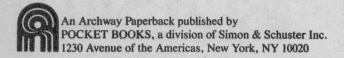

An Archway Paperback published by
POCKET BOOKS, a division of Simon & Schuster Inc.
1230 Avenue of the Americas, New York, NY 10020

ISBN: 0-671-64685-0

First Archway Paperback printing December 1988

10 9 8 7 6 5 4 3 2 1

DOUBLE EXPOSURE

Chapter

1

"BACON CHEESEBURGERS—they're the best," Joe Hardy said, licking a drop of sauce off his fingers.

Frank Hardy shook his head at his younger brother. "I don't see how you can eat that glop, Joe. Do you have a clue as to what that sauce is made of?" He pulled his own burger from the box on the car seat between them. "At least you know where you stand with a plain burger." He took a bite.

"Plain is dull," Joe said. "Like bland Mexican food."

"Plain meat"—Frank took another bite, waving his burger in front of Joe's hungry eyes—"and a plain bun." After downing the last of it, he swallowed contentedly and brushed crumbs off his jeans. "That's how the hamburger was made to be eaten."

"I'll only agree that it was made to be eaten,"

Joe said, leaning over the steering wheel. "Even if this guy never shows up, finding that burger joint made the trip worth it. Let's hit it again tomorrow night."

Frank checked his watch. Their contact was almost half an hour late. "Maybe I'll cook tomorrow night," he said. With their parents away on a fishing trip in Canada, and their Aunt Gertrude off visiting a friend, he and Joe had been eating out—and more often than not, they'd had junk food. Frank was beginning to feel unhealthy and bloated, but his lean, six-foot-one frame didn't show the effects of the past week's "diet." And Joe, though a lot broader than Frank, could hardly be called chunky.

"You? Cook? Please," Joe said, holding his hand over his mouth. "I just ate."

"Very funny," Frank said.

"Why can't Callie come over and cook for us?" Joe teased with a grin. "I think it's the least your girlfriend could do."

"I can't believe you said that, Joe," Frank told him. "Just because Callie's a girl doesn't mean she cooks."

"True," Joe said good-naturedly. "But she *is* a good cook."

"Hopeless," Frank muttered. "I'll throw this stuff out." He picked up the trash and stepped out of the van to look for a basket.

The street was empty and quiet, save for the slap of waves from the nearby bay. Frank shivered involuntarily, wishing that he'd worn something heavier than his windbreaker. The day had been sunny and warm, but fog and clouds had rolled in at dusk and the temperature had dropped.

They were parked in Bayport's old port section. Seventy years ago it had been a thriving waterfront district—but now, many buildings facing the piers were run-down and abandoned, the streets covered with litter, the sidewalks cracked with weeds pushing up through them, the docks themselves silent and bare.

Their father often told them this part of town was dangerous. And it looked it. But because of its reputation no one ventured there after dark, making it a perfect place for a secret meeting. Which is why our contact suggested it, Frank supposed. He caught sight of a dumpster about ten feet behind them and started toward it.

"Hey!" Joe called.

Frank turned at the sound. His brother was leaning out the side of the van, waving frantically. "Someone's coming!"

Frank looked. Sure enough, far up the street, he could see the headlights of a car cutting a dull yellow tunnel through the light fog. He threw up the lid of the dumpster, tossed his trash inside, and dashed back to the van.

"Action at last," Joe said as Frank slid into the passenger seat.

"Don't be so eager," Frank said. "I would

have thought that after our last escapade, you might want a bit of a rest.''

Joe smiled wickedly. "Not on your life."

Frank shook his head. Both he and Joe had nearly gotten killed in their last case, *Street Spies*, working undercover in New York City. But it hadn't stopped either of them from coming to this meeting. Like it or not, adventure was a way of life for the Hardy brothers.

"What could this guy possibly have that could clear Janosik?" Joe asked. "From what the papers are saying, it's an open-and-shut case."

"Don't believe everything you read," Frank said. Like everyone else, he'd followed the meteoric rise of Alexander Janosik, the Czechoslovakian dissident now living in the United States whom the papers had dubbed "the conscience of the Eastern Bloc countries." Now those same papers were saying Janosik had been paid by the CIA to make trouble for his native land. But Frank was standing by his original opinion of the man.

"You've seen him make those speeches, Joe," Frank said. "Do you think he said those things for money?"

"If it was a lot of money," Joe pointed out.

"Money isn't everything," Frank said. "What I'm wondering is why our contact wants to keep this meeting secret—and why he insisted on seeing Dad alone." The boys had been monitoring their dad's answering machine while he was away and decided this call was urgent and demanded their immediate attention.

"Well, we'll know in a second," Joe said. "Here he comes."

The headlights were inching toward them slowly—maybe ten miles an hour, Frank guessed, although he could barely see the car because of the fog and the glare of the headlights.

"Wow," Joe said, raising a hand to just above his eyes. He wanted to shield them from the glare. "Is that—yeah, it is." He nodded to himself. "A fifty-six Mercedes SL. You don't usually see one of those outside a museum." Joe was always fascinated by cars, especially expensive ones.

"Tinted glass," Frank noticed as the car nosed up next to them on Joe's side. The driver's window slid slowly down—and Frank and Joe found themselves face-to-face with one of the most formidable-looking men they'd ever seen.

Just sitting there, the guy gave off an aura of strength. Joe guessed he had to be over six feet, probably closer to six-six. Of course he could have short legs. But he had to weigh two hundred and fifty, judging by his beefy hands and the way his turtleneck strained across the muscles in his arms. His dark hair was clipped close in a way usually seen at army bases or prisons. But what truly made the man remarkable were his eyes.

His glance flicked over everything, but he seemed to look right through what he saw—as if the Hardys weren't any different from the Dumpster behind them. Those eyes turned people into things.

"Hi," Joe said hesitantly. Could this be their contact?

The man glanced at Joe, then Frank, then half turned his head to the back seat.

"Kids," he said in an accent Frank couldn't place.

The reply from the back seat was muffled, but its meaning was clear. Not even giving the Hardys a second look, the driver slid his window up and the Mercedes pulled away.

The brothers stared at each other. "Wow," Joe said. "Who was that?"

"Well, he wasn't our contact," Frank said, exhaling a breath he hadn't even known he was holding.

"I'm glad," Joe replied. "Talk about creepy."

"You can say that again," Frank said, leaning back. "Still—"

"What was he doing here?" Joe asked, anticipating Frank's question. "I hope we never find out."

Frank grinned and checked his watch again. "I don't think we're going to find out anything tonight. It doesn't look like our mysterious caller is going to show."

"Let's get back home then," Joe said, starting up the van. "We can rent a movie for the VCR, Callie can come over and make us some nachos—" He turned to Frank and smiled. "Just kidding."

Frank shook his head. "Hopeless."

Joe fastened his seat belt and checked the view in the van's mirrors. He reached out the window to adjust the sideview mirror.

A hand grasped his wrist.

"Don't be alarmed." A man had emerged out of the fog, leaning in through Joe's window. The upturned collar of his coat didn't give him much protection from the breeze that had come up. His sandy-colored hair was blowing across his forehead as he stared at Joe with gray, intelligent eyes. "You have blond hair." He spoke quietly, with the slightest trace of an English accent. "You must be Joe Hardy."

The man peered into the van. "And you have dark hair—so you're Frank." He shook his head. "I expected your father."

"He's away and we've been answering his messages," Joe said, his heart still racing from being startled by the man's sudden appearance. "How'd you know who we were?" he demanded.

"I asked Fenton to come, and two young men who resemble him have been parked here for an hour. I can add two and two."

Frank stepped out of the van and crossed around the front of it. Now that he was closer, he saw the man was younger than he'd first thought—twenty-five, maybe twenty-six. Though his manners were formal, there was a sparkle in his eyes as he studied Frank—almost as if he were looking at an old friend, instead of someone he'd just met.

"You said on Dad's machine that you have information that will prove Janosik is being framed," Frank said.

The stranger stared at him silently for a moment. "Yes," he finally said. "I suppose I should trust you, too." He smiled. "After all, we're family."

Frank raised an eyebrow. "What do you mean by that?" he asked. "Who are you?"

"Call me Chris," the man said. "I'm—"

Just then the van, the Hardys, and their contact were bathed in a blinding light.

"What?" The stranger turned, raising an arm to shield his face from the glare.

Blinded himself, Frank heard a car roaring toward them.

"The Mercedes!" Joe yelled.

Whatever it was—it was coming *fast*. It had to be doing sixty, Frank realized.

"What the—" Joe began.

A figure was leaning out the car window. As the Mercedes drove past, Frank saw that the person was holding a gun.

"Duck!" Joe yelled.

Gunshots rang out—a half dozen in quick succession.

Their contact spun around, then collapsed on the street.

8

Chapter

2

As soon as he heard gunfire, Frank flung himself down and rolled under the van. Another shot rang out, followed by the sound of glass shattering. Then the Mercedes roared past.

"Joe!" Frank yelled, scrambling to his feet.

The window on the driver's side had disintegrated. Joe, who had been looking out at Frank and their contact when the shots were fired, was nowhere to be seen.

Frank's heart was racing. Had his brother been hit? "Joe! You all right?"

Joe's head popped up in the shattered window as he brushed pieces of glass off himself. "I'm fine. But what's—" His words were cut off when he saw the contact sprawled on the ground.

"Oh, no!" Frank knelt beside Chris and reached inside his overcoat to check the wound. He pulled out an oblong plastic box, about the size of a hardcover book. It was completely shattered—though it still held the remnants of what had obviously been a videocassette.

Chris's eyes cracked open, and he moaned.

"You are one lucky guy," Frank said, opening Chris's overcoat all the way. The bullet had been deflected by the videocassette and had just creased the inside of his arm. It probably stung like mad—but he was alive. "He's okay!" he called to Joe.

Joe looked down the road. The Mercedes' taillights had been swallowed up by the dark and fog. "Well, I'm going to see if I can catch up with those guys," he said, revving the engine. "Nobody takes potshots at us and gets away with it!"

"Don't be a hero!" Frank yelled after him. "We'll call the police, and—"

He might have saved his voice. Joe had put his foot to the floor, and the van had already disappeared.

"No police," Chris said weakly, grabbing onto Frank's shoulder. His face was white; he was still in shock from the impact of the bullet. "Police—they can't handle—your brother will be killed."

"Take it easy," Frank said. "Joe can take care of himself." But remembering the Mercedes' driver, he had to admit he was a little worried.

Joe wasn't worried—he was mad. That was half the reason he was driving faster than usual down the two-lane winding coast road. The other rea-

10

son was that there were no exits on the road until the next town. He wanted to get the Mercedes in sight before it turned off.

Swinging out of a sharp curve, he found the Mercedes—parked directly across the road, blocking his path!

Joe slammed on his brakes and the van fish-tailed to a screeching stop inches short of a collision.

"Dumb, dumb, dumb," he told himself. "I should have guessed they'd know I'd follow them."

"Out of the van." Joe turned and saw the driver of the Mercedes advancing toward him, holding out a gun aimed directly at him. Out of the car, he looked even bigger than Joe had guessed.

"Now!" The man waved the barrel of his gun.

Joe stepped cautiously out of the van.

"Put your hands behind your back."

He did as he was told, keeping one eye on the man.

"Now," the driver said. "I don't know why you're following us, but I want you to remember one thing—I could have just killed you, very easily." He stared at Joe, his eyes cold and unblinking, seeing through him again. "I want you to remember just how easily."

He walked forward till the barrel was less than an inch from Joe's head. Then he cocked the trigger. "And now I want you to remember how important it is to stay out of other people's affairs, affairs that don't concern you. Will you remember?''

"I have an excellent memory." Joe met the guy's gaze coolly, waiting for an opening, any chance to disarm the man. "I certainly couldn't forget a face like yours, for instance."

The man's eyes narrowed. "I see that you may need a further lesson."

Joe smiled. "You may be right. But who is going to teach me?" He deepened his voice, mimicking the man's accent.

The guy's eyes flashed. "I would be happy to.''

Joe nodded toward the gun. "And do you need that to do it?''

Tightening his lips into a straight line, the man rammed his weapon into its shoulder holster.

"Gregor, no!" A small, balding man with wire-rim glasses and a loose-fitting suit burst from the back of the Mercedes. "I forbid it," he said, stepping toward them. "We cannot afford to—"

"Security is my department, Doctor," the man-mountain said. "Besides, this will only take a moment." He turned back to Joe. "Now," he said, balling his hands into fists. "Let's begin your lesson, shall we?''

Joe feinted quickly, then stepped back. He was pleased he'd gotten the driver—Gregor, that was what the other man had called him—to put away his gun. Now if he could just hold them there till Frank came with the police—

"Don't run away, my friend," Gregor said, moving toward him again. "How can I give you your lesson if you run away?" He took a half-hearted swing at Joe, trying to draw him closer.

He's big, all right, Joe thought, but he doesn't seem fast. Joe usually depended on his strength, not his speed, but Gregor was so much bigger than he was that Joe would have to use whatever advantages he had.

Seeing an opening, Joe darted left, tagging Gregor in the stomach with a hard right. Perfect!

But Gregor just stood there, smiling. "That is your best punch?"

Joe had a sudden sinking feeling in his stomach. That punch would have had anybody else doubled over, gasping for breath. Gregor didn't seem affected by it at all.

"Now let me show you my best," Gregor said. With that, he swung—much faster than he'd moved before, much faster than Joe would have believed possible for a man his size. He caught Joe square on the jaw. The force of the blow spun Joe around, and he pitched face forward onto the ground. He lay there, stunned.

Gregor stood over Joe, hands on his hips, staring down. "You are strong," he said. "But it seems you cannot take a punch. Perhaps you will need lessons in that as well."

Joe struggled to his hands and knees, trying to

clear his head. Suckered, he thought. He shouldn't have assumed that Gregor was slow just because he was big.

Gregor grabbed him by the neck of his sweat-shirt and hauled him to his feet.

"Let us finish this lesson first, though," he said, drawing back his arm.

Joe saw Gregor's fist, about the size of the moon, hurtling toward him till it filled his field of vision.

Then the world went black.

Someone was shaking his shoulder.

"Joe! Wake up!" It was a woman's voice. It must be his mother, trying to wake him up.

"I don't think I can go to school today, Mom," Joe mumbled. "I have a terrible headache." He turned onto his side. His mattress felt awfully hard. "Maybe I should go back to sleep."

"Do that, and you're likely to get run over." That was his brother's voice. "Frank?" Joe asked out loud. He opened his eyes.

He was lying by the side of the road. Frank was kneeling on one side of him, and Callie Shaw on the other.

"Oh, yeah," Joe said, rubbing his jaw. "Now I remember."

"Are you okay? What happened?" Frank asked, helping him sit up.

"The driver of that Mercedes had a hard right.

That's what happened." He looked at Callie. "How'd you get here?"

"He wouldn't let me call the police." Frank nodded toward Callie's car, which was parked by the side of the road. Chris sat in the back seat. "He said he'd tell us everything he knew, as long as we didn't bring the cops in. I asked Callie to come and get us, and we went looking for you."

Joe shook his head, trying to clear his thoughts.

"Did you get a license number?" Frank asked.

"No, it all happened too fast. But that shouldn't matter—that guy in the back of Callie's car has to know who they were." Joe wobbled to his feet.

"Take it easy, Joe," Frank said. "Give him a chance to catch his breath before you start interrogating him."

Joe waved his brother's concerns aside. "Relax—I have just a few simple questions for him."

He walked over to Callie's car. Chris looked up at him through the window.

Joe slammed his hand on the roof—hard. "All right, friend," he said, glaring at Chris. "Start talking. Who were those two guys in the Mercedes—the little man with the glasses and his king-size friend. And why were they shooting at you?"

"Easy, Joe," Frank said, laying a hand on his brother's arm. "He's hurt."

Chris climbed out of the car, rubbing a hand over his face. "I never meant for anyone to be hurt—especially you two." He set his jaw, and a muscle just above the bone moved in and out. "It's too dangerous—I should never have come here. I can't—I *won't* tell you who they are. They'll kill you!"

"They may do that, anyway," Frank pointed out. He laid a hand gently on Chris's shoulder. "You have to tell us who those men were."

Chris sighed and leaned back against Callie's car. He seemed to be deep in thought.

"All right," he said slowly, reluctantly. "Those men—I used to work with them. The man with the glasses is Dr. Finn Liehm. A scientist—and very brilliant."

"And the other?" Joe asked.

"That must have been Gregor Krc." He pronounced it *Kirk*. "They are both members of the Czechoslovakian secret police—what is called the STB."

"The STB," Joe said, smacking his fist into the palm of his hand. That explained the man's training at least. "But what're they doing here?"

"I think I can guess," Frank said. "It's something to do with Alexander Janosik, isn't it?"

Chris nodded but said nothing.

"Why'd you call our father for help? Who are you?" Frank said.

"Who am I?" Chris said slowly. He looked up and met Frank's questioning gaze. "My name is Chris Hardy."

Frank and Joe looked at each other. "Chris

16

Hardy?'' Frank asked. Joe just stared at him. ''Is that what you meant before—about us all being family? Are you related to us?''

''To your family—to you two especially,'' Chris said. ''You see, I'm your brother.''

Chapter

3

FRANK STARED at the computer screen in stunned silence. "I don't believe it," he said, shaking his head. "I just don't believe it."

He leaned back in his chair and rubbed his eyes. He'd been up since six that morning, trying to make sense of Chris's story. Now it was almost ten o'clock, and the only way things did make sense seemed as impossible now as it had the past night.

"Our long-lost brother," Joe had said when Chris first made his incredible claim, unable to keep the sarcasm out of his voice. "Come to claim the family fortune, I suppose?"

But Chris had ignored Joe's mocking comment and hadn't backed down. Without a word, he'd handed Joe his driver's license.

It was for one Chris Hardy, of 112 Smith Street, Northampton, Massachusetts. According to the license, Chris was twenty-six years old, stood

5'10" tall, and weighed 165 pounds. He had light brown hair and brown eyes. It was all there in living color in a smiling photo.

"So what if you have a license?" Joe asked, after they'd driven back to the Hardys' house and were standing on the walk before going in. "Do you really expect us to believe that you're our brother? I mean, why would our parents keep a secret like that?"

"I see they remodeled the front porch," Chris said, looking at the house.

Joe's mouth dropped open.

"How'd you know that?"

Chris smiled sadly. "I used to live here, too, you know." Then he'd reached into his wallet and handed Joe a yellowed, square snapshot—a shape not printed anymore. It was a picture of a young couple and a boy of not more than five or six, standing together on the Hardys' front porch—before it had been redone.

Frank had peered over his brother's shoulder to get a closer look. He recognized the couple immediately. Although they were a lot younger than he could remember ever seeing them, Frank knew it was a picture of his parents. And the boy? Although Frank couldn't swear to it, he did look a lot like Chris would have at that age.

"Photos can be faked," Joe had said. Of course, he was right. But after Callie had left, Chris told Frank and Joe things about their parents and relatives that he couldn't possibly have known, unless . . .

Unless he really was their brother.

He knew about Aunt Gertrude's secret passion of reading old mystery novels.

"And I'll bet she really loves this, too," Chris had said, pointing to the Hardys' VCR. "She can watch spy movies whenever she wants to now, right?"

Frank had smiled at that—Aunt Gertrude loved nothing better than to settle back in the couch, shut out the lights, close the door, and put a movie on the VCR. In fact, the more he talked to Chris and watched him walk around his house, the more he liked him.

Especially when he'd proven to be a computer buff as well.

"Nice," Chris had said, studying Frank's system. "Small, but very well thought out." Then he smiled. "I've got a different setup—a lot bigger. You're more than welcome to have a look at it."

"I'd like that," Frank said, smiling slowly.

"I'd like it better if you answered some of our questions now," Joe said, cutting in. "Like—"

"Can't they wait until morning?" Chris asked. "It's past two now."

Frank had been shocked to discover Chris was right—the time had passed very quickly. They'd all gone to bed, putting Chris in the guest room upstairs. Yet even though he liked Chris, Frank still didn't believe his story. So he'd gotten up early this morning, and, using access codes a hacker friend had given him, he'd logged on to the Bayport City Hall computer. He had expected the records to prove, beyond a shadow of a doubt, that Chris's story was false.

He'd gotten the surprise of his life.

Chris Hardy was real. But Frank couldn't call his mom and dad to verify it—they were deep in the wilderness.

"I don't believe it," Frank said again, shaking his head at the computer screen. "I just don't believe it."

He was looking at a notice of birth for one Christopher Edward Hardy, parents Fenton and Laura.

Frank pulled Chris's social security number and found a grade-school transcript for him—from the same school that both he and Joe had gone to. Chris had gone there until he was six and a half years old, at which point all trace of him disappeared.

About the time I was born, Frank realized.

He picked up Chris's driver's license for the umpteenth time and stared at it. All the details matched their contact perfectly. If it was a forgery, Frank had to admit it was the best he'd ever seen.

At eight-thirty this morning he'd even asked a contact of his at the Department of Motor Vehicles to check out the Massachusetts license.

She'd called back an hour later to verify that it was real.

He put the license down. None of this made any sense. He was getting a headache. And he was getting hungry.

The doorbell rang. It was Callie.

"Morning." Frank gave her a quick kiss at the doorway. "You look wide-awake and ready to face the day." She was wearing a pair of khakis and a bright green sweater underneath her jacket.

Callie looked him over and shook her head. "I hate to say what you look like."

"That bad, huh?" Frank tried to stifle a yawn. "I've been awake for a while—checking up on my new brother."

"Oh, Frank, come on," Callie said, hanging up her coat. "You don't really think—"

"Hey, what's all the racket?" Joe stood at the top of the stairs in his gym shorts and T-shirt, his wavy hair tousled into curls from sleep. "Don't you know there are people trying to sleep up here?"

"You're right—we'll try and keep it down," Frank said. "Chris's first night back home should be a restful one."

Joe and Callie both looked at him as if he'd gone crazy.

"What have you found out, Frank?" Callie asked.

He yawned again and stretched. "I'll explain over breakfast."

Joe came downstairs then and somehow convinced Callie to cook.

"Well, I'm still not ready to accept him into the family," Joe said, swirling his pancakes in a small stream of syrup.

Callie nodded. "Neither am I." She was sitting next to Frank on one side of the breakfast table, with Joe directly across from them.

"And I don't understand why you let him stay here last night instead of going to the cops," she continued. "You don't know anything about him."

"He knows a lot about us." Frank put his elbows on the table and rested his chin on his hands.

"Too much, I say." Joe grabbed the last of the pancakes off the platter set between them on the table. "Look, Frank—instead of proving who he isn't, let's just find out who he is."

"Has he told you anything else—about himself, his connection with those guys in the Mercedes, with Janosik?" Callie asked.

"We didn't find out much more about his connections with anyone. We got a little sidetracked last night with family history," Frank admitted.

"Well, I think it's time we got back on track," Joe said. "I owe that driver a thing or two—and they owe us for one new window on the van!" He carried his dishes to the sink. "I'll get dressed, and then we can have a little brotherly chat with our visitor." He smiled at Callie. "Thanks for the breakfast, Callie. You're a great cook."

Frank shook his head. How Joe had managed to talk Callie into making breakfast . . .

Callie turned and punched him playfully on the arm. "How come you never say anything nice about my cooking, Frank?"

Joe winked at him.

Maybe Chris *will* turn out to be my brother, Frank thought, watching Joe head for his bedroom. It's about time for a new one.

When Joe came back downstairs, he found Frank, Callie, and their friend Phil Cohen huddled around the breakfast table. The dishes had been cleared and put away, and what remained of the videocassette Frank had taken out of Chris's jacket the night before was spread across the table.

"The tape itself looks fine—all I have to do is splice it back together and put it in a new case," Phil was saying. He was slightly built with longish, dark curly hair and quick, deft hands. Phil was also Bayport's resident electronics genius. "Then it should be as good as new."

"We'll be really interested to see what's on it," Frank said.

"You think it might prove Janosik's innocence?" Callie asked.

"I hope so."

"Maybe it's an old home movie," Joe said, breaking into their conversation. "Hey, Phil."

"Hey, Joe," Phil returned the greeting. He swept up the pieces of the videocassette into a small case he'd brought with him. "Heard you had a little excitement last night."

Joe smiled. "A little," he said.

"So when do I get to meet this new brother of yours?"

Frank stood. "You'd both better let Joe and me talk to him first. He may be a little nervous."

The two brothers went upstairs to the guest room. "I don't care how nervous he is," Joe said, knocking heavily on the door. "We need to start getting some answers."

There was no answer from inside.

"Chris? You in there?" Frank called.

He turned the knob slowly. The door swung open.

"I don't believe it," Frank groaned.

Joe slammed his hand against the wall.

The blankets lay on the floor. The sheets had been rolled tight and tied together. One end was knotted around the bedpost. The other hung out of sight—out the window.

Chris was gone.

Chapter

4

"SO MUCH FOR ANSWERING all our questions in the morning," Frank said, surveying the room.

Callie and Phil joined them after hearing Joe's outburst. "So what are you going to do now?" Callie asked. Frank pulled the sheets back into the room, untied them, and bundled them up in his arms.

"I think Joe had the right idea before," he said, leading them all downstairs and dropping the sheets in the laundry. "Find out who Chris really is."

"And how are we going to do that? We still don't know anything about him!" Joe protested.

"We do know one thing—where he lives."

"Right—if the address on his license isn't a fake," Phil pointed out.

"We can check with the phone company to see if he's listed there," Callie said. She picked up the phone.

"You could also try to find out more about Krc and Liehm," Phil suggested. "Maybe the Czech embassy knows something about them."

"About the STB?" Joe shook his head. "Not very likely."

"And they wouldn't tell us if they did," Frank said. "Espccially if those two are involved in a plot to smear Janosik."

Callie hung up the phone. "There is someone named Hardy in Northampton on Smith Street," she said. "But the number's unlisted."

"Which leaves us with only one way to find out if it's Chris," Frank said. He turned to Joe. "Can we take the van?"

Joe frowned. "I had to take the window on the driver's side off completely."

"You'd better get it replaced if we're going to drive all the way to Massachusetts," Callie said. "The weather report said it might rain."

"What do you mean, 'we'?" Joe asked. "This case may be too dangerous for you."

Frank nodded. "I'm afraid Joe's right, Callie."

Callie glared at both of them. "Forget what I said about getting that window replaced. You're both all wet already!"

"Ouch," Joe said, shaking his head. "I'll check the repair shops."

It took them almost an hour to find a shop that could replace the window, and another five hours of steady driving before they reached the outskirts of Northampton. They had stayed off the big interstate highways and stuck to smaller roads, which made for a more scenic drive if a longer one. By the time they drove into Northampton, both of them were anxious to get out and stretch.

"Hey," Joe said, pointing ahead. A huge shopping mall sprawled on both sides of the road. "Let's stop and get something to eat before we look for Chris."

Frank yawned. His lack of sleep was beginning to catch up to him. "I guess I could use a cup of coffee."

They locked the van and entered the mall.

"All right!" Joe pointed to a sign ahead that said, "Humongous Hamburgers." He grinned. "I see what I want!"

"You go ahead," Frank said, catching sight of a coffee shop. "I'll meet you back here."

He strolled over and stood in the entrance for a moment. The coffee shop was empty, except for a waitress who sat on a stool at the far end of the counter. Her back to the door, she was counting out change and watching a small black-and-white television set.

Frank walked in. "Excuse me," he called.

The clatter of a fresh handful of change from her apron drowned out his voice.

Frank walked toward the counter. He was about to tap her on the shoulder when he noticed a newspaper lying in the last booth. It was a

Boston paper—the *Tribune*—and it was opened to the international page. The headline had caught Frank's eye: "Bum Czech?" The byline was Jean Eykis's. He read on.

"Alexander Janosik, the noted Czechoslovakian dissident, will deliver the keynote address at a special Harvard symposium on Saturday. Janosik, whose vigorous opposition to the repressive policies of the Czech government has made him a hero here and in Europe, has recently been accused of accepting money from the CIA in exchange for his anti-Czech speeches. Exclusive sources have promised to provide this reporter with proof of Janosik's guilt before he addresses the symposium on Saturday."

The waitress looked up. "Sorry, hon, I didn't see you there. Did you want something?"

"Never mind," Frank said, bolting out the door.

He found Joe talking to a tall, pretty, dark-haired girl outside the hamburger shop.

"I don't get up here too often," Joe was saying, "but maybe if you give me your number, we could—"

The girl laughed.

"Excuse me," Frank said. He grabbed Joe by the arm. "We're leaving."

"Hey, wait a minute," Joe said, trying to plant his feet. "What's the big rush?"

"Duty calls," Frank said.

29

"You'll have to excuse my brother," Joe said. "But look, if you're ever in Bayport—"

"I'll know who to avoid," she said, turning around and flouncing off.

Joe watched her walk off and sighed heavily. "You're ruining my life, Frank."

Frank ignored Joe's comment and told him what he'd just read.

"But Chris promised us that Janosik was being framed." Joe shook his head. "Where is this reporter going to get proof of his guilt? From Liehm and Krc?"

"Maybe," Frank said. "What we need right now is information. Let's try Chris first. Come on."

"Smith Street," Joe said, turning off the main road onto a quiet, residential block. The houses lining the street were old and small, but they looked well kept. Children were playing in one of the front yards.

"A nice enough neighborhood," Frank said. "There's number one-twelve." He pointed to a brick house with a postage-stamp garden about halfway down the block on the right side.

They drove past it slowly. "That's the one," Frank said. "The mailbox says C. Hardy."

"Our first lucky break," said Joe, parking the van. "Let's see if he's home."

They crossed the lawn to the front door, and

Joe rang the bell. Frank peered in through the front window. "I don't see anyone," he said.

"And nobody's answering the bell." Joe pushed the buzzer again and then pressed his ear against the door. "I can't hear anything, either. It must be broken." He knocked heavily on the front door—and it swung open.

Frank knelt down beside the door and examined it. "The lock's been smashed."

Joe stepped past him into the house. He groped around for a light switch, found one, and flipped it on. Frank heard him breathe in sharply. "That's not all that's been smashed around here. Take a look at this!"

Frank followed him in. They stood in a small entranceway. Directly ahead of them was a staircase. To their right was the living room, which now looked like a disaster area.

Furniture had been overturned and thrown around the room, papers and books strewn across the floor, and the carpet had been ripped up from the floor in several spots.

"Wow," Joe said quietly. "Someone wanted something pretty bad."

"Here's something they didn't want—something that proves this is Chris's place, anyway," Frank whispered, picking a picture up off the floor and showing it to Joe. It was the same photo Chris had shown them last night, the picture of himself and their parents.

Joe tapped Frank on the shoulder and pointed

down the hall under the staircase. A light shone from beneath a door at the end of the hallway. "I think somebody's in there!" he mouthed.

They tiptoed down the hall runner, and Frank put an ear to the door.

"Someone's in there, all right," he said directly into Joe's ear. "I can hear papers rustling."

"What are we waiting for, then?" Joe whispered back. "Maybe it's Chris."

"It's probably whoever wrecked the house," Frank replied. "Let's do this carefully. We'll go in one at a time."

Joe nodded. Without waiting for Frank, he burst into the room.

Someone was standing in front of a desk with his back to the doorway, going through some papers. He turned when he heard Joe enter.

"You!" the man said, looking astonished.

Joe was almost as startled as he was. It was the guy from the back seat of the Mercedes.

"You know him, Joe?" Frank asked, stepping in behind his brother.

The man reached into his jacket, yanked out an automatic, and pointed it at the Hardys. "I don't know what you two are doing here, but I will most certainly call the police if—"

"Good idea," Joe said, stepping to the left side of him. Frank moved to the right, circling the man. They both began to move closer.

"Yes, why don't you?" Frank chimed in. The

man's gaze darted back and forth between them.

"Stay where you are, or I'll shoot!" he said nervously.

Joe smiled at him. "Just take it easy, Doctor," he said soothingly. "No one's going to shoot anyone. Why don't you just put the gun down, and—"

In one swift motion, Frank's foot lashed out, striking the man's hand. The gun went skittering under the desk.

"Now," Joe said, putting a hand on the man's chest and pushing him back until he sat in the desk chair. "This is the guy who was in the back seat of the Mercedes," he said to Frank. "The driver called him Doctor—Doctor Liehm, Chris said."

Frank stared down at the man. "Maybe you can help us by answering a few questions."

"There is nothing I can tell you," Liehm said.

"Would you rather that *we* call the police?" Frank asked. "I'm sure they'd be interested in talking to you about that mess out there and the broken lock, to say nothing of the shooting last night, and—"

A wide smile spread across the doctor's face. "Talk to *him*," he said, lifting his chin and looking behind the Hardys.

Joe turned and saw Gregor filling the doorway behind them.

"Perhaps I can help you find what you're looking for," he said, advancing on the brothers.

Chapter

5

As FRANK TURNED to face Gregor, Liehm grabbed the phone from the desk and slammed him over the head with the handset. Frank dropped to his knees.

"Frank!" Joe cried out. He turned on the doctor, who shrank back into the corner, then back toward Gregor.

Gregor raised his fists. "This time, I will make sure you do not wake up."

Gregor feinted with his left, then threw a hard right at Joe, but now Joe knew how fast he was. He dodged back and to the right, letting his left leg follow through and slam Gregor in the side. The man grunted in surprise and pain.

Joe followed with a hard right that caught Gregor full in the face. Blood begin trickling from Gregor's nose. Joe stepped back.

Out of the corner of his eye, he saw Frank struggling to his feet.

Gregor wiped his face and saw the blood on his hand. He looked at Joe with equal amounts of amazement and fury. "No one ever—" he began, his teeth clenched. "For this, you will die!"

"No, Gregor!" Joe turned to see Liehm had retrieved his gun and was holding it on both him and Frank. "Enough—the last thing we need is another murder."

Gregor ignored him. "They know too much," he said, advancing on Joe. "We must make sure they tell none of it—ever."

"Stop!" Liehm pleaded, gesturing wildly with his gun. For a minute Joe thought he might shoot Gregor. "You'll ruin the entire plan!"

Gregor halted and was silent for a moment, as he considered what Liehm had said. Finally he spoke. "All right, Doctor. We do not kill them—this time."

Joe helped Frank to his feet. He could see his brother was still dazed.

"But we will have to ensure they do not follow us," Gregor said, assuming control of the situation again. "There is no evidence here of our presence?" he asked.

"None," Liehm said.

"Good. Hand me the gun, please."

Liehm did so, slowly and uncertainly. He was terrified of what Gregor might do, Joe realized.

"Good," Gregor said, smiling. "Now—there is some rope in the kitchen. Please bring it to me."

Liehm seemed about to protest, then marched off.

"You get along well with everybody, don't you?" Joe asked.

Gregor ignored the taunt. "A very messy weapon, a gun," Gregor said, studying the barrel. "I usually prefer other ways of dealing with my problems." He smiled, revealing large white, even teeth. But the glint in his eye made him look anything but friendly. "I promise you this, though: if I see you again, I will not hesitate to use this gun."

Joe wanted to reply, but the edge in Gregor's voice and the intensity on his face kept him silent. There was no sense in goading Gregor just now.

Joe promised himself he'd find a time to settle matters between the two of them—when there was no gun separating them.

Liehm returned with the rope. Gregor took it, and tied the Hardys' hands and feet—quickly, efficiently, and very tightly. When he was done, Frank and Joe were sitting back to back in the middle of the floor, securely bound.

"Better." Gregor nodded, admiring his work. "Much better." He smiled down at them. Then he calmly kicked Joe very hard in the side. Joe gasped. Gregor kicked him again—harder—then knelt at Joe's side, staring directly at his face.

"Who are you, boy? Why do you follow me?"

Joe gritted his teeth and said nothing. He stared straight ahead, ignoring Gregor's gaze.

"No smart words now, eh?" Gregor asked. He pulled Joe's wallet from his pocket, flipped through it, and frowned. "Joe Hardy."

"Hardy?" Liehm echoed, surprise in his voice. "Are you related to Chris?"

Joe started to say no, but Frank's voice stopped him.

"He's our brother—I'm Frank Hardy," he added.

"What has he told you about us? He never mentioned any brothers to me."

"Shut up, Doctor," Gregor said, tossing Joe's wallet on the floor next to them. He ripped one piece of cloth off an overturned couch, then another, and used them to gag the Hardys.

He knelt down beside them again. "You follow us to avenge your brother—admirable." He shook his head. "But stupid. Don't do it anymore." He stood and turned to go, but stopped at the door.

"Remember what I said." He met Joe's eyes. "Because the next time I see you, I *will* kill you."

The door slammed shut behind him.

It took Frank and Joe almost an hour before they were free.

"That's another one I owe that Gregor," Joe said, gingerly touching the spot on his side where Gregor had kicked him. He felt the bruise starting to form already.

"Did you notice Gregor said 'avenge your brother'?" Frank asked, getting to his feet and stretching. His head still hurt where he'd been slugged with the phone. "They think they killed Chris."

"Well, that's an advantage for him," Joe said. "I only wish it was one for us."

"So what were they looking for here?" Frank asked.

"The videotape Chris had with him?"

"That's a good guess," Frank said. "But I don't see a VCR. Or a computer, for that matter. Remember when Chris told me I should see his system, because it was so big?"

Joe nodded. "Yeah. So where is it?"

"Maybe he keeps it somewhere else." Frank went to the desk they'd found Liehm rifling through and began looking through some papers. "Here's a stack of printouts—and an electric bill from a few months ago for over a hundred dollars! You don't pay that kind of money to keep your refrigerator running. That equipment's here somewhere."

They searched the house from top to bottom but found nothing. Finally, they retraced their steps to the front hall and surveyed the wreckage in the living room.

"Maybe Gregor and Liehm found his equipment and took it," Joe said.

"I don't think so," Frank said. "I think they decided there wasn't anything here." He walked through the living room slowly, studying the over-turned furniture, the scattered papers, the ripped carpet. Finally, he stopped by a section of bare wood floor the torn carpet had exposed. He knelt down, staring intently.

"What is it?"

"Am I crazy, or does the wood here have a lighter varnish than that in the hall?" Frank asked, pulling up more of the carpet. He looked at Joe. "Give me a hand with this, will you?"

They peeled back the entire carpet to the right of the staircase till an area about ten feet square had been exposed.

Joe nodded. "This whole section of the floor is new—but so what?"

"I'm not sure." Frank paced back and forth several times between the living room and the front hall, stopping to gaze up the staircase and then back at the exposed floor.

He snapped his fingers.

"A basement," he said.

Joe looked at him. "A basement?"

Frank nodded. "That's where Chris's equipment is."

Joe scrutinized the floor carefully. "You mean a trap door? I don't see anything."

"Maybe not," Frank said. "I think they moved the whole staircase to cover it."

"Sure," Joe said, shaking his head. "I think you've been watching too many spy movies."

"No, look." Frank stood squarely in the center

of the brighter section of floor. "The stairs used to start here, and took a ninety-degree turn halfway up. All they had to do was knock out the old basement entrance, and swing that bottom half of the staircase around to cover it."

" 'All they had to do.' " Joe shook his head and stared at Frank dubiously for a minute. "All right," he said. "So there's a hidden basement. How do we get down there?"

"Simple enough," Frank said. "There ought to be a hidden entrance." He walked around in front of the staircase again and reached below the edge of the first step. "Aha!" he said, lifting up. The first six steps were hinged; they raised up to reveal a set of stairs leading down.

Frank grinned up at Joe's frowning face. "Just like in the spy movies." He held the entranceway up for his brother. "See if you can find a light down there."

Joe took several tentative steps down the dark stairway. "Got it," he said. Frank lowered the hinged steps, and followed him. Joe stopped on the bottom step.

"You're not going to believe this till you see it," Joe called up.

Frank joined his brother on the bottom step and caught his breath.

The basement was filled with electronic gear. There were five separate computers, two large-screen televisions, four videotape recorders, and several machines he barely recognized at all.

"This is incredible," Frank said. "There's more computer memory down here than in our entire school." He moved to one of the unfamiliar machines and hesitantly touched it.

"One of the new laser imagers," he said wonderingly. "I didn't even know they were on the market yet." He touched another next to it. "And this modem—it's even more advanced than the one we have at home."

Joe stared. The modem on their computer system didn't just let them use telephone lines to communicate with other computers. It was a highly sophisticated piece of gear, to keep them in contact with the Network, a supersecret government agency.

"I think this is what Gregor and Liehm were looking for."

"But what's it all for?"

"Beats me." Frank took another look around the room. "It's not your standard business computing setup, or anything like that. No one would need all this video equipment." He walked around and finally sat down in front of one of the computers with a keyboard. "Let's try asking the machine what it's doing here."

He switched the machine on and began typing commands into the computer. Joe came and stood behind his shoulder.

Frank shook his head. "He's got the whole system keyed to a password."

"Are you trying to guess it?"

"That would take forever. No, I'm trying to bypass his program and talk to the machine directly." He typed instructions too fast for Joe to understand. Suddenly the screen lit up.

Frank grinned. "We're in," he said. Joe clapped him on the shoulder. "Now let's find out what he's got on file here."

He called up a directory and let the names of the files scroll by. Nothing looked familiar, until—

"Hold it!" Joe said. "What's that one say?"

"I see it," Frank replied. " 'Janosik'—and it's not just one file, it's a whole directory of them." He called up one of the files onscreen. A whole array of symbols appeared.

"This is weird," Frank said, studying the monitor. "I don't know what this is—looks like a very complicated series of printing commands."

"What does it mean?" Joe asked.

"I don't know," Frank said. "Let's try another file." He called up one called "Itinerary."

"At least this one's in English," Joe said. The screen showed a listing of place names and times.

"Yeah," Frank said, reading off the screen. " 'Arrive Hotel Charles—' " He shook his head. "Let's look at the other one again for a second." He called up the directory again and stared at it for a moment.

"Hey!" Joe exclaimed. "What's going on? What are you doing?

42

The list of files in the directory was shrinking, disappearing one by one.

"I'm not doing anything," Frank said. "Someone else is in the system—and destroying all the files!"

Chapter

6

"Do something! Stop it!" Joe yelled.

"I'm trying to!" Frank frantically typed in new instructions to the computer. Before his eyes, the files were disappearing.

"What's happening?"

"I don't know—maybe I triggered some kind of self-destruct program, or—" He glanced up quickly and looked across the basement. "No! It's got to be the modem! Somebody must be tying in by phone and telling the computer to erase these files!" He dashed across the room, Joe a step behind him.

"Can we stop it?" Joe asked.

"That's what I'm trying to do," Frank said, staring intently at the modem. He knelt behind it and found the wire connecting it to the main system.

"Here it is," he said, holding the wire in his

hand. "If I disconnect this, we should be able to cut off whoever's on the modem."

Joe stared at him. "Well, what are you waiting for?"

Frank hesitated. "We may not only disconnect the modem, we may crash the whole system. That way, we'll lose all the files."

Joe yanked the wire out of Frank's hand. "We're definitely going to lose them if we don't."

Frank nodded.

Joe pulled the wire free.

Across the room, the monitor went suddenly dark. The computer made a soft humming noise that gradually faded away, like a car running out of gas. Then the basement was completely silent.

Joe cleared his throat and looked at Frank questioningly. Frank shook his head. "I think—"

"Don't say it," Joe said, leaning back against a wall of equipment.

Frank sighed. Whatever had been in the computer, whatever Chris had known about Janosik—all that information was gone.

"There's nothing more we can get here," Frank said. Joe nodded reluctantly.

They went upstairs again, carefully lowering the stairs on the secret entrance to Chris's basement.

In spite of all the equipment in the basement, they'd found nothing—no computer disks, no videocassettes, no records of any kind—to indicate what had gone on there. Erasing the computer's files was apparently the last step in a very thorough housecleaning operation.

"Nothing is what we've got," Joe said in disgust.

"Not quite," Frank said. He picked up the phone and dialed. "Yes. I'd like the number of the Charles. It's a hotel in Cambridge." He covered the mouthpiece with one hand. "Let's check and see if that little bit of itinerary we saw was really Janosik's."

Lifting his hand, he spoke into the receiver again. "I see—yes, thank you, operator." He hung up quickly and looked at his watch. 10:00. Not too late to call.

"I'm going to see if he's there," he told Joe, dialing the number the operator had given him.

"This is the Charles, Bonnie speaking. How may I help you this evening?" The woman who answered had a distinct Boston accent and the efficient, practiced voice of a well-trained receptionist. The Charles was clearly a classy hotel.

"May I have Mr. Janosik's room?"

"Ah—yes, one minute please." A note of uncertainty crept into her voice. "I'll connect you." Frank recognized the hesitation and covered the receiver again. "Something's going on," he told Joe. "They put me on hold."

Joe moved in closer and stood by his side, leaning over his shoulder to listen in on the conversation.

The next voice that came on the phone was not

the receptionist's, but a man's—deep, powerful, and authoritative.

"This is Lieutenant Considine—to whom am I speaking, please?"

"I'm sorry. I was looking for Alexander Janosik." Frank mouthed the word *police* to Joe.

"How did you know Mr. Janosik was staying here? Who is this?"

Frank replaced the receiver quietly. He didn't have anything he could tell the police—yet.

"He's there, all right."

Joe nodded. "We ought to be there, too."

"I think you're right, but we have to take care of a few loose ends first."

They phoned the local police anonymously to let them know that Chris's house had been broken into, and climbed in the van to start the long drive back to Bayport.

No sooner had they gotten onto the highway than it started to rain—lightly at first, then harder. The rhythm of the raindrops beating on the windshield and the swish of the wipers as they cleared the glass quickly lulled Frank to sleep, and he didn't wake up until they were almost home.

"How are you doing?" he asked Joe, peering out through the windshield. He could barely see the road, it was raining so heavily. "Want me to drive?"

"No, it's all right," Joe said. "I'm fine." He

paused for a moment. "Who do you think was on the other end of that modem? Chris?"

"Probably," Frank said, stifling a yawn. "But why would he destroy his own information?"

"Because there was something in there he didn't want anyone to see," Joe replied. "Something that connected him with Gregor and Liehm—maybe what they were going to use to frame Janosik. Maybe after he ran away from us, Chris got cold feet about turning them in."

Frank was silent for a moment. What his brother was saying made sense. He wanted to like Chris, but more and more, it was impossible to see his role in this as innocent.

"Frank?" Joe asked quietly. "You don't really think he's our brother, do you?"

"Of course not," he said, trying to hide the lingering doubts in his voice. Watching the road ahead of them flash by, he thought of the birth certificate he'd seen that morning and the smiling young man who had seemed so comfortable in their house.

He shook his head. "It's impossible."

They finally got home at three in the morning and found a small package waiting for them in the mailbox.

"I'll bet I know what this is," Frank said, holding it in his hand. "Chris's videotape, in a brand-new case, courtesy of Phil Cohen."

He unlocked the front door and stepped inside,

turning on the hall light. Joe rushed in behind him, running to escape the downpour.

"Whew—that's the hardest it's rained in a long time!" Joe said, taking off his coat and kicking off his wet shoes.

"It'll be good for Mom's garden," Frank said, hanging up his own coat.

"If you like vegetables." Joe blew on his hands and walked toward the kitchen. "How about some hot chocolate?"

"Sounds good." Frank ripped the package open. It was the videotape, with a brief note from Phil.

"Frank/Joe," it read. "Here's the tape. Part did get damaged—about two seconds, total. I watched it. Call me tomorrow after you do. Phil."

Frank smiled. "It's the tape, all right. I'll go slip it in the VCR."

"Be there in a minute," Joe called back.

Frank went into the den and turned on the TV, then the VCR. He checked that the tape was rewound to the beginning and inserted it in the machine.

A minute later Joe walked into the room carrying two steaming mugs of cocoa and handed one to Frank.

"Thanks," he said, sitting back on the couch and taking a sip of the hot chocolate. Joe sat down next to him.

"Now," Frank said, picking up the remote

control and setting the VCR to Play. "Let's see what's on this tape."

At first they saw nothing but snow—no signal at all. Then the screen turned black and some letters appeared.

" 'Janosik Project—DD Insertion'?" Joe read aloud.

"Beats me," Frank said, shaking his head.

The letters cleared, and for a moment there was static again. Then a picture appeared.

On the screen, it was winter—outdoors, in a rural area. Two men, one old, one young, both wearing army uniforms, stood on the steps before a large white frame house. They were talking, but the tape had no sound.

"Those are Russian uniforms!" Joe exclaimed.

Frank nodded. Something about the scene seemed terribly familiar. "The older one's a colonel, but the picture quality is really terrible. I'm surprised. With all that video equipment Chris had . . ." His voice trailed off.

On the screen the two men were arguing now. The older man's face betrayed confusion and surprise. He gestured angrily.

The younger man's face became frozen, an expressionless mask. Without betraying what he was about to do, he raised a gun. The older man fell backward down the steps of the building, his blood staining the snow.

Frank turned white and leaned forward, spilling his hot chocolate on the couch.

Joe's eyes widened. "Frank—that soldier . . ."

Frank nodded, his mouth suddenly dry. He rewound the tape till he reached a single closeup of the young soldier, then pressed Freeze-Frame on the remote control.

The face on the screen, the man who had shot the older officer—

It was Chris.

Chapter

7

"YOU'LL GO to the police now, right?" Callie asked Frank. It was the next morning, and she was sitting in the Hardys' den, facing Frank.

"Wrong." Frank released the Freeze-Frame button on the remote control and rewound the videotape. He'd watched the shooting too many times since last night.

"Yeah," Joe said, walking out of the room and returning with two suitcases. "We're not going anywhere—except where we're going." He smiled.

"Which is Boston and Cambridge," Frank said. He took Callie's hand and smiled reassuringly. "We don't have anything to tell the police. What would we say? We may have witnessed a tape of a murder in Russia? If we go to Boston, we'll be near Janosik, we'll be able to talk to that newspaper reporter, and we'll—"

"Be right in the line of fire if Chris decides to shoot Janosik, too!" Callie said angrily.

She leapt up and began to pace the room. "Frank, he's *not* what he pretended to be. He's a killer—a member of the Russian army, maybe even the KGB! What if those two guys from the Czech secret police—whatever their names are—"

"Krc and Liehm," Joe said.

"Right—what if they're trying to stop Chris from killing Janosik? Did you think of that? What if they're the good guys?"

"If they're good guys, I'll never eat a burger again," Joe said. He stood in front of Callie. "Take a look at this." He lifted his shirt, revealing an ugly bruise that practically covered one whole side of his body. "Good guys don't kick you when you're tied up."

"I don't think they're on Janosik's side," Frank added. "And we don't know whose side Chris is on. But I think you're right about one thing—Alexander Janosik's life could be in danger."

"So we're flying to Boston," Joe said. "We want to make sure that Janosik is safe."

"And how are you going to do that?" Callie asked. "You told me the police wouldn't even let you talk to him on the phone. Once that symposium begins, you won't be able to get near him."

"We'll manage," Frank said. The doorbell rang. "Come on in—it's open!" he yelled.

"Hi, everybody," Phil Cohen said, walking

into the room. "You're all set." He handed Joe a piece of paper. "Go to this address and ask for the Beast. He'll get you into Janosik's symposium."

Callie threw up her hands in defeat.

"The Beast?" Joe asked, his eyes widening as he studied the note. "What kind of name is that?"

"He's a friend of mine," Phil said defensively. "I don't know his real name—I just exchange messages with him on a computer network. He goes to Harvard and knows how to do things with computers I'd never even think of trying."

"How's he going to get us into the symposium?" Frank asked.

Phil shrugged. "I didn't ask. And I don't want to know."

Joe grinned. "Good enough for me." He picked up the suitcases. "Come on, Frank, we've got a plane to catch."

Frank turned to Callie. "We'll be staying at the Charles."

"You're going to stay *there?* Frank, that's the most exclusive hotel in Cambridge! How are you going to afford it?"

"Oh, we'll figure out a way."

"Maybe the Beast can help you," Callie suggested wryly.

"He probably could," Phil offered. "Once he told me about the time that he—"

Frank smothered a laugh. "We'd better catch that plane."

The plane ride was uneventful. They arrived at Boston's Logan Airport in late morning and took a cab to Cambridge, emerging into an early-September afternoon.

"This is Harvard," Frank said as they walked through an open gate in the fence that surrounded the "Yard," the old part of Harvard's campus. "That's the Quad, where all the dorms are." He pointed straight ahead, then stopped to take a jacket out of his bag and slip it on. It had been unseasonably cool the past week.

"Wow," Joe said, studying the beautiful old campus and ivy-covered buildings. "This is really great."

Frank smiled and took a long look around. Everyone walking by seemed to be a student—not much older than they were.

But they were at Harvard for reasons other than sightseeing. "Come on," he said to Joe. "What's that dorm where Phil's friend is?"

"The Beast." Joe shook his head and pulled the note out of his pocket. "Columbus—building F."

They stopped a campus security guard and asked him for directions. He pointed off to the left. "Columbus," he said. "It's a whole new set of buildings back that way. You can't miss it."

"Thanks," said Frank. He and Joe followed

the instructions. The buildings they passed were all hundreds of years old, four- and five-story brick dorms, classroom halls, a Greek-looking building with the single word *Philosophy* carved above its door.

For a second Frank felt as if he and Joe had traveled in time—perhaps to some ancient English university like Cambridge or Oxford. But when they came to a group of squat, modern three-story buildings, they were definitely back in the present.

"There," Joe said, pointing to a building in the middle. The door was locked, so Joe rapped loudly on it.

A girl opened it. "Yes? Can I help you?" she said. She was beautiful, and when her eyes met Joe's, she gave him a dazzling smile.

Joe gulped but said nothing. Frank gave him a quick poke with his elbow.

"Oh—ah, yes, we're looking for someone named—the Beast," Joe said, clearing his throat.

The girl's face fell. "Corner room all the way down the hall." She held the door open to let them pass. "Just follow your nose."

"Phil's friends are loved everywhere," Joe said, watching her walk away. They found the corner room. Frank set down his suitcase and knocked on the door.

It opened a crack. This time, it wasn't a beautiful girl who answered, but a slight young man. He looked about fourteen, and had short blond hair and wire-rim glasses. His T-shirt said Computers Are People, Too. And drifting out of his room came the odor of stale popcorn. "Who are you?" he asked, peering at them suspiciously.

Frank exchanged a glance with Joe. "We're looking for the Beast. Phil Cohen sent us—we're Frank and Joe Hardy."

"Oh." The little blond student squinted up at them and nodded. "That's me—I'm the Beast."

Joe did a double take. "You? The Beast? You don't look like a beast." In fact, he added silently, you don't look old enough to be in high school, much less college.

"I know, I know," he said, pushing his glasses back up on his nose. "My real name is Larry— Larry Biester—so they call me the Beast. Hold on a minute." He shut the door.

Joe looked at the pages of computer printout that were plastered across the face of the door, and then looked at Frank. "The Beast."

Frank nodded. "The Beast."

When the door reopened, Larry emerged and handed Joe an envelope. "These'll get you into the government symposium—it's over at the JFK Center, across campus."

"Thanks," Joe said. Beyond the Beast's shoulder, he could see a dark room, dominated by a flashing computer terminal and to the side of it a pyramid of empty soda cans.

"Okay," the little guy said and shut the door so fast it almost slammed.

"Wow," Joe said. "And I thought high school was strange."

"Yeah," Frank nodded. "Maybe college isn't such a good idea after all."

The guard they'd gotten directions from before told them where the JFK Center was, and they found it without much trouble. It was an entire group of buildings, combining classrooms, offices, and a research library. They also found something else.

"The Charles," Joe said, pointing to a building on the hill behind the JFK complex.

"Where Janosik is now," Frank said. He stared at the large, fenced-off construction area that spread between the campus and the hotel. "Looks like they're building a parking garage here."

"When does the symposium start?" Joe asked.

Frank studied the announcement schedule on the center's bulletin board. "According to this, today—continuing over the next three days. Janosik doesn't speak till Saturday, though."

Joe continued to stare up the hill at the Charles. "You know what I'm thinking? Maybe we should go to the hotel, register, dump these bags, and find Janosik. Tell him what we know."

"Good idea," Frank said. "We can also call that reporter—Eykis—and see what she's got that proves Janosik was being paid by the CIA."

They followed the sidewalk up the hill to the

Charles. It was a huge building, sprawled across the top of the hill and down one side, all the way to the Charles River. Its ground floor was a series of restaurants and shops, tailored for Harvard's visitors.

The lobby itself was so overcrowded that at first Frank had trouble spotting the registration desk. Finally he saw it at the far end of a long corridor lined with stores. He and Joe made their way to the desk.

"Hi," Joe said to one of the six or seven women behind the long desk. "We'd like a room for tonight, please."

She didn't even bother to look down. "I'm sorry, sir, we're totally booked through the weekend."

"Oh, no!" Joe leaned over the counter and tried to look horrified. "Couldn't you please double-check—isn't there anything?"

The girl leaned over her computer terminal. "I'll see if there are any last-minute cancellations," she said doubtfully. Joe waved Frank over to the desk, not so much because he thought she might find them a room, but so that Frank could see what she was doing on the computer.

"No, nothing," she said. She smiled at them. "There's a motel down the street you might try."

"Thanks," Joe said. "Could we leave our bags here for a couple of hours?"

The girl started to say no. But Joe smiled his most winning white-toothed smile, and she nodded and pointed to a spot beside the desk. Then Joe and Frank walked out of the lobby.

"There was an office around back," Frank said. "I'll bet there's another computer in there. All I have to do is get on that reservations systems for a minute, and I'll have the best suite in the house."

"It'll have to be later," Joe said, studying the crowd. "When this place clears out." He brightened. "Let's go down to the river and check it out."

He stopped suddenly as he realized Frank was no longer walking beside him. His older brother had halted a few paces back, staring to the left.

"What is it, Frank? What's the matter?"

"There," Frank pointed. An elderly man sat on one of the benches in the courtyard in front of the hotel, engrossed in reading a book. "That's Janosik!"

He and Joe walked toward the benches and sat down next to him.

"Alexander Janosik?" Frank asked.

The man looked up from his book slowly, staring at Frank. His hair was almost entirely white, and his deep-set eyes were friendly. Heavy bags under them made him look as if he hadn't slept in years.

"Yes, I am Alexander Janosik. Who are you?" Unlike Gregor or Liehm, his English was almost entirely unaccented.

"My name is Frank Hardy, sir. This is my

brother, Joe—but we're not important right now," he began. "Mr. Janosik, I have reason to believe your life could be in danger. Have you ever heard of two men named Krc and Liehm?"

To Frank's surprise, the man began to laugh. "Heard of them? Yes, I have, young man—but I'm quite safe. I have some very qualified people watching over me."

"Really?" Joe, amazed at Janosik's disregard for his safety, moved forward. "Like who?"

"Like me." Suddenly a large black man towered over them. "Move away from him—now!"

Chapter

8

FRANK AND JOE STOOD CAUTIOUSLY.

"Please, Lieutenant," Janosik said. "These young men are harmless enough, surely."

"Let's see some ID," the man said, ignoring Janosik.

Frank tried desperately to think of what to do—and then remembered the envelope that the Beast had given them. He handed it to the man.

That should buy them some time to think of a story, at least.

"What's this?" The security man tore the envelope open and pulled out two cards, scrutinized them and then looked at Frank and Joe.

It was over, Frank realized. He started to look for a way to explain that they only wanted to help Janosik, but the man interrupted him.

"Why didn't you say you were grad students?" he asked, handing them back their cards.

Frank looked at his. There was his picture—on

a Harvard graduate student ID. He looked at Joe, who was studying his card with the same apparent confusion.

"Oh, ah—yes. The program today was particularly interesting," Frank said. "That's all we wanted to tell Mr. Janosik."

"I thought I heard you say something about his life being in danger." The security man stared hard at Frank. "Your voice is very familiar—and the name Hardy rings a bell, too."

"Please, Lieutenant Considine," Janosik said. "They are merely students—and it is young people that I am most interested in talking to."

Considine! Frank thought. He answered the phone last night when I called. He tried not to look nervous as the lieutenant studied him.

"All right," Considine said finally.

"Thank you." Janosik carefully marked his place in the book he was reading and stood. "Perhaps you two young men would like to accompany me on a walk through the park down there?" He pointed past the hotel in the direction of the river.

"We'd be honored," Frank said.

Joe nodded. "You bet."

"All right, then." Janosik smiled.

"My men will stay close behind you." Considine motioned, and two men who had been inconspicuously studying hotel shop windows moved forward. "Have a nice walk, Mr. Janosik."

Frank and Joe flanked Janosik as he started down the hill, the two men following.

"So," Janosik began. "You know Liehm and Krc. I am surprised. You seem a little young to be traveling in their circles."

Frank smiled. "We sort of stumbled in."

"Let me give you some advice, young man—stumble back out. They are dangerous men."

"It's you we're worried about," Joe said.

Janosik laughed again, more harshly. "Me? Liehm, Krc—they cannot hurt me." He shook his head. "I am dead already."

Frank and Joe exchanged startled glances, but Janosik offered no explanation.

They came to the end of the hotel grounds. Two marble pillars stood flanking the entrance-way to a small park. Each was engraved with quotations.

"These are the words of your President Kennedy," Janosik said. "You are too young to remember him—but he was a great man."

Frank nodded and said nothing.

"The world was full of great men in those days," Janosik said, staring at the words on the pillar. "Kennedy, his brother Robert, Martin Luther King, Dubcek, Svoboda—" He shook his head as if to clear it and smiled at the Hardys. "Those last two names mean nothing to you."

"No," Frank admitted. "I'm afraid they don't."

Janosik slowly traced the outline of the engraved quote with his hand. When he finally spoke, his voice was strained and harsh.

"They were the leaders of my country in 1968, the year King and Kennedy's brother were assassinated. Now they have been erased from our history books." He turned to the two young men at his side. "Alexander Dubcek tried to reform our government, to give the people a voice in their own affairs, to give socialism a human face, as your western press said."

"What happened?" Joe asked.

"He failed," Janosik said curtly, striding past the pillars and into the park. There was a fountain in the center, with benches carved into the marble around it. More quotations from President Kennedy were engraved on the marble surrounding the fountain.

Janosik sat on one of the benches and continued his story. "The Russians invaded my country. On the night of August twentieth, 1968, their tanks crossed our borders." He shuddered. "Their troops filled our streets. They kidnapped our leaders and dragged them back to Moscow, tried to force them to submit to the Kremlin's will, make them renounce the changes they had begun.

"They held them for seven days, but Dubcek would not yield." His voice shook with remembered anger. "He would not yield! And the country stood firmly behind him. We gave the Russians nothing!" He was silent for a moment, then pointed at the quotation carved into the marble in front of them, and began reading from it.

" 'When at some future date the high court of history sits in judgment on us . . . our success or failure in whatever office we hold will be measured by the answers to these four questions: Were we truly men of courage? Were we truly men of integrity? Were we truly men of judgment? Were we truly men of dedication?' "

Frank watched Janosik read those words, and it was as if the old man were somewhere else, reliving the most important moments of his life.

"For seven days—and several months beyond—the people of Czechoslovakia were all those things, and more. Then it ended. The reforms were repealed. Husak"—he spat the name—"came to power. And men like Liehm and Krc emerged from the sewers they'd been hiding in to frighten my country into silence once again."

He sighed heavily. "I sometimes wonder what would have happened if John Kennedy, or his brother, had been president in 1968. Maybe they would have stopped the Russians. Maybe I—and my country—would still be alive."

He turned to Frank again. "It does not matter what they do to me—I am as one dead and have been for more than twenty years. I continue to speak out so the words of men like Dubcek are not forever lost. So that what happened to Czechoslovakia never happens again."

Janosik gave them a tired smile. "But you two are young, you have your whole lives ahead of you. Don't risk them trying to save me." He nodded at Considine's men, who stood at the edge of the fountain. "That is their job."

He stood. "Now if you'll excuse me, I must return to my room. I grow tired." He nodded in farewell and shuffled slowly out of the park. Considine's two men followed him out.

Frank watched him go. "Still think he's being paid by the CIA?" he asked Joe.

Joe shook his head slowly. "Forget I ever said that."

"I don't care what he said—I'm not letting anything happen to that old man."

"Me, either," Joe said.

The boys were suddenly famished and went in search of lunch. They found a pizza place, which made Joe happy, although he did end up having to pay for the whole thing.

"Didn't I buy dinner the other night, too?" Joe asked.

"You did," said Frank. "And don't think I don't appreciate it."

"Very funny," Joe said. "I'm keeping track, you can bet on that."

Frank didn't bother to point out that Joe had already spent most of the money they had for the entire week on hamburgers.

When they returned to the Charles, it was

midafternoon, and the lobby was much less crowded. The same young woman was on duty at the registration desk and smiled sadly when she saw them approaching.

"I'm afraid we're still all booked up," she said.

"I thought you might be," Joe said. "But I really came back to ask you about that motel, I couldn't find it anywhere. Do you think you could show me where it is?" He gave her his most charming smile.

"I'm sorry—I can't leave the desk," she said.

"I could watch it for you," Frank volunteered. "If anyone comes, I'll direct them to one of the other registration clerks." Frank smiled at the long line of women identically dressed in blue suits. They all seemed to be enjoying a joke and weren't paying any attention to the boys.

The young woman studied their faces carefully. "All right," she said finally. "Come on," she said to Joe. "I'll point it out for you."

Her place was at the end of the counter, and Frank stood and watched them walk out of the lobby. It was easier than he'd expected. He reached over with his left hand and idly logged on to the terminal. The women were still occupied with their stories, and Frank just appeared to be waiting for someone. First he found Janosik's room, and then he quickly discovered that the suites adjoining it on either side were being held empty. He logged on a reservation for himself and Joe in one of them.

He finished in just a couple of seconds. "It really is just up the road—I don't know how we could have missed it," Joe said.

"Then we're set," Frank said, nodding at Joe and picking up his bag.

When they got outside, Joe turned to Frank. "So?"

"We're in," Frank said. He smiled. "But we'll have to be very quiet."

When their reservation clerk went on break, they simply approached one of the others and checked in.

"Easy enough," Joe said, tossing his bag on one of the two beds in their room. "Now what?"

"Now we try that reporter—the one who said she was going to get proof of Janosik's guilt."

"Jean Eykis, you said."

"Right," Frank said, picking up the phone. They put him through quickly when he called the newspaper, and he made an appointment to see her in an hour.

Joe frowned. "Shouldn't one of us stay, and keep an eye on Janosik?"

"He really made an impression on you, didn't he?"

"No," Joe said defensively. "I just don't like the idea of leaving him alone here, without one of us watching him. I'm not too impressed with his police protection."

"Okay," Frank said, checking his watch. "I'd

better get going. You stay here—I'll go talk to Jean Eykis.'' He opened the door and checked the hall for any sign of Lieutenant Considine or his men. The coast was clear.

"And remember," he told Joe. "Be quiet."

Their room had a TV, so Joe spent the next couple of hours switching back and forth between various programs. But there wasn't anything worth watching, so he eventually got bored and shut it off.

He stood and crossed to the window. Outside it was still bright daylight. He had a view of the courtyard in front of the hotel and the street beyond.

Cambridge, like every other city he'd ever been in, had at least one problem in common with all other big cities—too many cars, and not enough parking spaces. Right now, on the street below, Joe could see some kind of fight taking place over a space.

A man stepped out of one car and leaned through the window of the other. Whatever he said to the driver made that car give up the fight for the space and speed away.

Joe smiled—then he looked closer.

The car now pulling into the parking spot was the silver Mercedes that had shot at them two nights before!

Chapter

9

JOE REALIZED THE DRIVER had to be Gregor, and he watched the Mercedes for a moment, his mind racing. Should he warn Janosik? Or Considine? Where was Liehm?

Then he heard the sound of loud, angry voices coming from the room next door. He leaned up to the wall and pressed his ear against it.

"What threats you make! I will not be silenced!" That was Janosik's voice—more passionate than it had sounded earlier in the park. Joe had to smile. Maybe Janosik thought he was dead to the world, but he sounded very much alive.

"Come, Alexander, be sensible." Joe knew that voice, too. Liehm. "We do not require you to stop speaking entirely. All we ask is that you stop making these foolish speeches against our government, and our friends, the Soviets."

"Nothing you can do will make me stop speaking against those invaders!" Janosik said.

"Oh?" Liehm asked. "Let me show you this." There was the sound of furniture, or something heavy, being moved in the next room.

"Watch closely, Alexander."

Joe strained to hear but was unable to make out what was happening. They had stopped talking completely.

Then Janosik spoke again. "This is not how it happened—not at all. I met with them, yes—but I never took money."

Liehm laughed—a cruel, barking sound. "Who is to say how it really happened? All that is important is that the television stations will have this tomorrow—unless you change your speech."

Janosik's reply, when it came, was quiet and subdued. "I need to think."

"Fine. I give you until this evening at ten. If I do not hear from you by then, I will release the tape to the TV stations." The sound of moving furniture came again. "Goodbye, Alexander." Liehm's voice was mocking. Joe heard Janosik's door open, then shut again.

The tape? What was going on here? Joe moved from the wall to his door. He cracked it open to watch Liehm walk slowly down the hall to the elevators, carrying a large suitcase.

What could Liehm have shown Janosik that would make him think about changing his speech? Joe had to find out. He had to follow Liehm.

Grabbing his coat off the bed, Joe dashed into the hall. He raced down the three flights of stairs and outside into the courtyard. There was the Mercedes—and Gregor. He itched for a chance to confront him, but Liehm would be coming out of the elevator in a minute. He had to find a way to follow them. If only he had a car . . .

Just then a young boy raced past on a skateboard, and Joe barreled after him.

"Hey, kid!" Joe yelled.

The boy turned.

"I need to borrow your skateboard," he said.

"Borrow?" the boy asked. He looked Joe up and down. "Get real. I don't even know you."

"All right, all right," Joe said. He saw Liehm moving through the hotel lobby and turned his face away. "I'll buy it from you. How much?"

The boy sized Joe up. "I paid a hundred bucks for this skateboard, mister."

"A hundred bucks?" Joe's eyes widened. He didn't have that much on him. "For a skateboard?"

The boy smiled at Joe. "A hundred bucks— take it or leave it."

Joe glanced around. Gregor had gotten out of the car to put Liehm's bag in the trunk. Liehm was sliding into the back seat.

"All I have is a twenty," Joe said desperately. "Twenty to rent it—how about it?"

"Rent it?" the boy shouted indignantly. "You trying to cheat me or something?"

At the curb Gregor turned to see what was happening. His eyes met Joe's, just before he reached into his coat.

"Duck!" Joe yelled, throwing his arm across the kid and dropping to the sidewalk, putting himself between Gregor and the boy.

Gregor pulled out his gun and fired. The bullet clanged off one of the courtyard benches. He'd used a silencer—a couple of people looked up but saw no cause for alarm.

Gregor fired again. Joe rolled behind a bench, still shielding the boy. The bullet slammed into the walkway, spraying them with chips of cement.

This time someone saw. "He's got a gun," a woman screamed. Gregory holstered it and climbed into the Mercedes. The car screeched off down the street.

The boy looked up at Joe with wonder in his eyes. He wasn't even scared, Joe saw. None of this was real to him.

"Wow," the boy said. "Are you a secret agent, or something?"

"Or something," Joe said, brushing himself off. Gregory was getting away, and he couldn't follow.

"Well, why didn't you say so?" the boy asked. He pointed at his skateboard. "Take it."

Joe smiled at the boy. "Thanks—I'll return it."

He climbed on the skateboard and started to roll uncertainly down the sidewalk, slowly at first, then picking up speed. He hadn't been on a skateboard in a couple of years.

"Go get 'em!" the boy cheered, raising his fists and shouting.

"Gangway," Joe yelled as he wobbled down the hill.

People dodged from the path of the obvious maniac, letting Joe keep the Mercedes in sight. The car came to the bottom of the hill and turned right—into heavy traffic. Joe knew he'd be able to keep up with a car caught in traffic.

Then he saw the sidewalk ended at the bottom of the hill. Joe gulped. Taking a deep breath, he jumped the curb and landed smack in the middle of traffic.

Joe leaned wildly to his left, then right. He was going to fall. He was going to get run over.

Desperate, he grabbed onto a truck in front of him to steady himself. He clung to it like a drowning swimmer to a life preserver, until he'd regained his balance.

Joe looked up and smiled. He'd managed to latch onto a vehicle two cars behind the Mercedes. If they stayed off the highway, he'd be able to follow it wherever it went.

Of course all that depended on how long he could keep his balance and whether the truck turned off.

*   *   *

Frank held out his hand. "Jean Eykis?"

"That's right." The woman in front of him smiled and shook hands firmly. She looked in her midthirties, with long dark hair and a square, pleasant face. "And you are—"

"Frank Hardy," he said. "I was hoping to talk to you about Alexander Janosik."

The woman nodded. "I have very little time, but you said you had some information for me?"

Frank pulled up a chair next to her desk. They were in the middle of the newspaper's city room. Dozens of people occupied the single room, some dropping off copy on the many desks around him, while others were typing in front of small computer monitors attached to all the desktops.

"What do you have for me?"

Frank decided to take the direct approach. "What makes you so certain that"—he tried to remember her exact words—"'Alexander Janosik has been accepting money from the CIA for his anti-Czech speeches?'"

She frowned. "Why are you so concerned?"

Frank leaned forward. "I think he's being smeared—and I think you're being used."

Her lips tightened. "A strong accusation."

Frank nodded. "I realize that. Who are your sources for this information?"

"You know I can't tell you that," she said.

"A man named Liehm—or Krc, perhaps?"

Her eyes widened, and she stared at Frank, surprised by his knowledge.

"They're with the STB—the Czech secret police. How I know this isn't important," Frank quickly continued. "But I have to know if they gave you anything—you said that you were promised proof positive of Janosik's guilt."

Eykis continued to stare at Frank—then shook her head. "You're either on the level, or . . ." Her voice trailed off. "They promised me something tomorrow morning. And that's all you get."

Frank smiled.

"With the STB, you said?" Eykis repeated. "You're sure?"

"As sure as I am of anything right now," Frank said. "Do you have a way to get in touch with them?"

"Why should I give away that information?"

"Because your story's not true," Frank said simply.

She laughed. "All right. I may kick myself in the morning for doing this, but—Liehm did give me a number." She rummaged around her desk. "Let's see—here it is."

She copied it onto a piece of note paper and handed it to Frank. "If they really are STB, that would explain why they're so anxious to see me announce Janosik's guilt." Jean Eykis gave Frank a concerned stare. "And if they really are STB, you shouldn't be fooling around with them."

Frank stood. "I'll be careful."

"All right, Frank," she said, getting up as well. "And I'll have some of my sources check on

Liehm. I'm not anxious to print this story unless it's true—I've been an admirer of Janosik's for years.''

"Thanks," Frank said. "And good luck—you can reach me at the Charles if you need to."

"Good luck to you, too."

He went downstairs to a phone booth and called Joe. No answer. Maybe Janosik went out, and Joe followed him. In that case, he was on his own for a while. He decided to dig a little more, dialing the number Eykis had just given him.

No answer there, either.

If only he had a way to find the address to go with that number—he'd have something. If he were home, he'd be able to tie in to the telephone company's computer. . . .

But he didn't need his computer at home to do that. Not when there was someone here in Boston who could supposedly do anything with a computer.

The trip back to the dorms took only a few minutes.

"Beast!" Frank banged on the door loudly. "Open up!"

A rustling noise came from inside the room.

Frank hit the door again. "Come on, Beast."

The door creaked open slowly. The little blond guy, in a long nightshirt and slippers, appeared at the door, staring at Frank. "Who are you?"

"Frank Hardy—don't you remember? Phil Cohen's friend."

"Oh." The Beast nodded. "Need some more ID?"

Frank shook his head. "No—I'm sorry to bother you, but it's important." He handed him the phone number. "Can you get me an address to go with this?"

Beast yawned and took the slip of paper back into his room, shutting the door behind him. A moment later he emerged and handed Frank another slip of paper.

"This is it?"

"That's it," the Beast said, yawning. "I'm going back to bed now."

Frank started to say good-night, but the door closed in his face.

Going back to bed. Frank looked at his watch. At five o'clock?

He shook his head.

College was going to be weird.

Joe was lucky—not only did the Mercedes stay off the highway, but the truck that he'd attached himself to stayed with the Mercedes till it pulled off the road and into a parking garage near the center of Cambridge.

He let go of the truck and glided silently to a halt across the street from the garage. Gregor and Liehm left the garage and entered the lobby of the building next door. As they entered, a uniformed guard waved a hand in greeting, and all three crossed to the back of the lobby and disappeared into an elevator.

Joe tucked the skateboard under his arm, crossed the street, and entered the building. While waiting for the elevator and its operator to return, he studied the building directory.

Apparently there were few tenants. One whole floor was occupied by Rehearsal Systems, Inc. Another floor belonged to a firm named Video Imaging. There was a copying firm, a collection agency, and an exercise studio as well.

"Hello? Can I help you?"

Joe turned and found himself facing the elevator operator, a young man not much older than he was. He smiled.

"Yes—maybe you can. The two men you just took up—I saw one of them drop his wallet in the garage next door. I'd like to return it."

"Sure, come on in." He let Joe enter the elevator first, then followed and shut the door. "That's very nice of you. Not many people would turn in a wallet."

Joe shrugged. "No big deal."

"Oh, but it is," the operator said. "I'm sure there are some important papers in that wallet. Their company does a lot of important work."

"Oh?" Joe asked, trying to appear casual. "What kind of work?"

"I think it's something to do with television— they're called Video Imaging."

"Video Imaging," Joe repeated, keeping his

voice calm. Their first real break! Now maybe he'd be able to start figuring out how Janosik, Liehm, Gregor, and the mysterious disappearing Chris Hardy tied together.

All he had to do was find a phone—Frank should be back from his meeting by now—and they were in business.

"Here you go," the operator said, opening the door. "They're at the end of the hall."

"Thanks," he said, stepping out of the elevator. "I can take it from here."

"Oh, no, Mr. Hardy."

Joe turned, and saw the elevator operator holding an automatic on him.

"Dr. Liehm and Mr. Krc would never forgive me if you got lost on the way." He smiled. "They're waiting for you."

Chapter

10

FRANK HUNG UP the phone again, concerned and puzzled. There was still no answer at their hotel room. What had happened to Joe? Where had he gone?

He stood by the phone booth on the corner and looked down the block. The address the Beast had given him was for an office building. It seemed ordinary enough. But somehow he felt the answers to a lot of the questions he and Joe had been facing these last few days were in there.

He was dying to check it out—but he wasn't going in alone. That's the kind of stunt Joe would pull. He always leapt before he looked.

This part of Cambridge was almost entirely commercial and almost entirely deserted now that it was after five o'clock.

The ground-floor stationery stores were all locked up, and the delicatessens and restaurants were closing up.

At that moment a flicker of movement in the alleyway between the building and the parking garage caught his attention. He pressed back against the wall and looked closer.

There was a man at the service entrance of the building, trying to force his way in!

Frank crossed the street quietly and made his way toward that alleyway, sticking close to the storefronts and staying out of sight. He reached the end of the last building and peered around the corner.

Apparently, the intruder was having no luck. The service door was resisting all his efforts to force it open.

There was something familiar about the man, about the way he moved. Then he turned slightly, giving Frank a quick look at his face.

Frank stepped out into the open, unconcerned about the noise he made now. The man spun around, startled, and almost dropped the tools he'd been using.

For a moment they stared at each other. It was hard to tell who was more surprised.

Then Frank spoke. "Hello—brother."

Chris Hardy said nothing.

"Hardy? Me?" Joe asked, studying the man's face and the way he held his gun. He was a professional, too—probably STB. Definitely not an elevator operator. "I'm afraid you have the wrong guy, mister. And what's with the gun?"

"Please." The operator shook his head tolerantly. "Don't insult my intelligence. Mr. Krc saw you following them on that ridiculous toy"—he indicated the skateboard—"and told me to make sure you didn't get lost on your way up to see them." He motioned Joe forward with his gun.

"All right, but you're making a mistake." Joe threw up his hands, as if he were going along quietly, then suddenly he flung the skateboard at the man's gun hand. The gun went off with a loud crack and flew halfway down the hall. He followed the skateboard with a left that caught the STB man square on the jaw and sent him reeling backward.

He had to get out of there and fast. That gunshot would bring everyone else on the floor running. He started for the elevator, but the operator grabbed his arm and spun him around.

Joe threw a quick right, but the man ducked and circled behind Joe to block his path to the elevator. Then the STB man pivoted swiftly on his right foot and aimed a karate kick at Joe's head.

Joe ducked under it and grabbed the man's foot as it passed over him. He intended to use it as a lever to swing him around. But the agent kept his balance, and swung his other leg under Joe, cutting his knees out from under him. Both fell to the floor.

They rolled over and over, each trying to get on top of the other. There was a flurry of blows—

and then the STB man had his hands tight around Joe's throat and was forcing the breath out of his body.

With his last bit of strength, Joe rammed his knees into the man's chest, lifting him up and over and slamming him into the far wall with a loud crack.

"Whew." Joe struggled to his knees, gasping for breath. The other man didn't move.

Someone clapped. "Very nicely done, Mr. Hardy."

Joe groaned. He recognized that voice.

Liehm stood over him, two other men flanking him. Both were holding guns on Joe.

"And now, if you would please accompany us"—he smiled—"Mr. Krc is very anxious to see you."

Slowly Chris let his hands drop to his sides. "I shouldn't be so surprised you managed to find this place." He forced a smile. "Actually, I'm glad you're here."

"I didn't think I'd ever see you again," Frank said. He studied the tools Chris had dropped. Now that he was closer, he could see that they were electronic gadgets. It seemed as if Chris wasn't using force to get into the building at all. "What are you doing?"

"I'm disarming the building's—Liehm's—security system," Chris said. "It's quite sophisticated.'' He picked up his tools again. ''I can stop them, here, tonight—with your help.''

''Not so fast,'' Frank said, grabbing Chris's shoulder and turning him so he was looking directly into his eyes. ''A friend of mine pieced together that videotape you were carrying. We watched it last night. Who was that man you shot?''

Chris shook his head slowly but said nothing.

''And who are you? What country do you work for?'' Frank asked.

Again, Chris shook his head, avoiding Frank's eyes.

Frank exploded. ''Why don't you tell us what's going on? First you come to us to help you prove Janosik is being framed—then you run away before we can help you!''

''I didn't come to you for help!'' Chris yelled back. ''I came to your father!''

''Well, you got us,'' Frank said angrily. ''And you'll find that once Joe and I start something, we like to finish it. Now, what's this all about?''

Chris took a deep breath. ''I've been waiting across the street all day for the chance to disarm and get inside this building,'' Chris said. ''Earlier Liehm and Krc went out. I thought the others would leave soon.''

''Others?''

''The other employees of Liehm's company— the other STB agents here. But they haven't left yet—and now Liehm and Krc have returned.''

He looked Frank directly in the eye. "Joe followed them in half an hour ago. He hasn't come out yet."

Frank turned white. "Joe followed them in—alone?" He was too concerned for his brother to be angry at him.

"I didn't see him until it was too late to stop him," Chris said. "Now, are we going to disarm this system and go in there, or do you want to ask me any more questions?"

In answer, Frank picked up one of the electronic gadgets and carried it over to Chris. "Okay," he said, grim determination in his voice. "Show me how to use this."

"I said I would kill you, and I will—make no mistake about that." In contrast to the last time Joe had seen him, Gregor was calm and in complete control of himself. He paced slowly back and forth in front of Joe, who was sitting in a chair with armed guards standing on either side.

They were in the company's security center. A long console covered with television screens split the room in half. The screens were tied in to cameras hidden throughout the building. Joe hadn't expected to find this level of technical sophistication—but that wasn't the only surprise he'd gotten at Video Imaging.

The first had come after Liehm led him through dozens of offices to this room. The equipment around him exactly duplicated that which he and Frank had found in Chris's basement.

He hadn't been able to put all these pieces of the puzzle together yet—but the picture was getting clearer.

"I will not have you interfering in our plans again. I want to know everything you and your brother know." Gregor stopped pacing directly in front of him and rested his palms on the arms of the chair Joe sat in. He leaned forward until their faces were barely six inches apart. "Tell me, and I promise you a painless death."

Joe shook his head. "That doesn't sound like much of a bargain to me."

"Where is your brother now?" Gregor asked.

Joe stifled the urge to ask which one and merely smiled.

Gregor shrugged as if to turn away—and backhanded Joe hard across the face.

"I do not like you, boy," he said. "I do not like looking over my shoulder and finding you there." He snapped his fingers. One of the guards handed him a gun. He pointed it at Joe. "Answer my question—where is your brother?"

Joe shook his head. He tasted blood running from a cut in his lip. "I honestly don't know."

Gregor studied the gun in his hand. "I said before I didn't like using this as a weapon." He smiled and cocked the trigger. "Perhaps in your case I will make an exception. . . ."

Joe shut his eyes.

"No, I forbid it!"

Joe cracked an eye open. Liehm had entered the room and stood beside Gregor, one hand on his arm.

"We cannot keep committing murders, Gregor—not in this country."

The taller man removed his finger from the trigger and pressed his lips tightly together, trying to control himself. "Yes, Doctor," he said, lowering the gun slightly. "What would you have me do?"

Liehm smiled. "Be patient, my friend. All our plans will triumph, very soon." He reached for the gun in Gregor's hand.

Gregor swung his arm around viciously, catching Liehm full in the face with the butt of his gun. The doctor fell to the ground as if he'd been struck by lightning.

"Patience?" Gregor roared. "Patience is for weaklings, Doctor."

Liehm stirred slightly. Gregor reached down and hauled him to his feet. "I will let you continue with your ridiculous, expensive scheme because Prague has ordered me to. But it is I who am in control here, I who will deal with this intruder. Is that clear?"

Liehm nodded feebly.

"Now do what ever you need to do!" He shoved Liehm, and the doctor stumbled out the door.

Gregor turned his attention back to Joe.

"Wait a minute, I thought you were on the same side."

"We are," Gregor said. "But I disagree with the doctor's methods. He will be satisfied to ruin Janosik's name—as if that would silence the traitor forever. But there is only one way to make sure one's enemies are truly silenced." He smiled at Joe and raised the gun, pressing it to Joe's head.

"This way."

Chapter

11

JOE SHUT HIS EYES.

He heard a loud, almost deafening noise.

Then another. And another.

He opened his eyes.

The security center was in a state of frenzied activity. Alarms were going off everywhere.

"What—?" Gregor said, turning away from Joe. "What is happening?"

"A break-in, sir—downstairs!" One of the men who had been guarding Joe was now hunched over a security monitor. "Unable to isolate the location!"

"Doctor!" Gregor yelled, striding out of the room. He turned back and pointed at Joe. "Keep an eye on him!"

The guard not watching the monitor leveled his gun at Joe. Gregor returned with Liehm. The whole right side of the doctor's face was swollen.

Gregor motioned him over to the security monitor. "What is this taking place? Why don't we see anything on the cameras?" he asked.

Liehm's fingers ranged over the controls expertly, and the cameras began moving, their view changing on all the screens.

"There!" Gregor pointed. "Downstairs, at the service entrance." He turned to Joe and smiled. "It looks as if your brother has decided to join us."

Joe sat up. Sure enough, there was Frank, apparently trying to force a door downstairs.

Liehm shut off the alarms, but continued to work the console. "This is strange," he said. "I can't get the cameras to move any farther."

"What is the matter?" Gregor asked. He pointed to the two guards. "You! And you! Go downstairs, escort our friend back here. He'll want to see his brother."

The two guards left, and the man Joe had met earlier, who had been posing as the elevator operator, walked in.

"What is it, Ludvik?" Gregor asked.

"The tapes—should I send them now, Doctor?" Ludvik asked Liehm. "Or do we wait till morning?"

Liehm shrugged and said nothing.

"Doctor?" Ludvik pressed.

"Send them now—it doesn't matter," Gregor said, smiling. "One newspaper and two television stations—and they all think they have an 'exclusive.' Yes—send it."

92

Ludvik nodded and left.

"Something is wrong with this monitor, Krc!" Liehm insisted. "Someone has tampered with it!"

"Nonsense, Doctor." Gregor came and stood by his side. "I have been here the whole time."

While they were talking, Joe made a move as if to stand up—and Gregor, still talking to Liehm, shook his head.

"I wouldn't do that, Mr. Hardy," he said, pulling out his own gun again. "You'll miss your last chance to see your brother—breathing."

Joe sat down, disgusted. How had Frank managed to find this place? And why was he breaking in alone? Why hadn't he brought along any backup? He shook his head. It didn't sound like Frank. It sounded like him.

Gregor called his attention back to the monitor. "I want you to watch this."

On the screen, Frank, who had been attaching something to a cable running along the outside of the building, suddenly looked up from what he was doing. The two guards moved into the picture, guns held high. Frank raised his hands, and for a minute, he looked directly into the camera.

Then the screen went dark.

"What has happened, Doctor?"

"I don't know!" Liehm's voice was both angry and frustrated. "I tell you, something is the matter with this machine!"

Gregor frowned. "Perhaps," he said. "We will

wait till the guards return, and run a check on the system.''

Gregor paced the floor anxiously, while Liehm stood silently by the security console. Five minutes had gone by.

"I do not understand this!" Gregor said. "Where are they? They should have been back long ago!"

Joe shrugged and said nothing, but inside he felt a tiny spark of hope flicker. "Maybe somebody offered them a better job," Joe suggested.

Gregor shot him an angry look and was about to say something.

Then the alarms went off again.

"Another break-in!" Liehm said, studying the console, confusion in his voice. "In two places at once!" If his run-in with Gregor had punctured his self-confidence, his inability to make the security system work had clearly shattered it.

"Calm yourself, Doctor!" Gregor said. "Shut off the alarms, and isolate the break-ins." He frowned at Joe. "Clearly, your brother is a lot cleverer than you are. Somehow, he has managed to turn our security system against us."

Liehm complied with Gregor's orders. "The break-in is again at the service entrance and our private staircase," he said.

"I will go myself, this time," Gregor said. He handed Liehm his gun. "Watch him. Do not leave this room. His brother may be leading us all on a wild goose chase. If I do not find him, I will return in five minutes."

"Wait!" Liehm said. "What if you don't come back?"

"Then you will be in charge again, Doctor." Gregor smiled. "You can do what you like."

As soon as Gregor left the room, Joe leaned forward in his chair. "He's going to kill Janosik," Joe began.

"Shut up!" Liehm yelled. "Do you think I don't know that?"

He raised his gun. "Bring that chair over here—that's it." He positioned Joe against the wall, keeping the console with its rows of TV monitors between the two of them, so he could watch both. "Now sit down, and be quiet!"

Joe decided not to test Liehm any further. Clearly, the man was on the verge of cracking up.

Now that he couldn't see the monitor screen he had no way of judging what was happening downstairs. He remained still in his chair, listening intently for any sound.

Five minutes passed quickly, and Liehm grew more agitated, more concerned. "What's happening out there?" He slammed his hand down on the console. He turned to Joe. "Where is everyone?" he demanded.

"Here I am, Doctor."

Both of them turned to see who had spoken. Chris stood framed in the doorway.

"You!" Liehm said.

"I'll bet you never thought you'd see me again," Chris said, walking into the room. "Hello, Joe."

Joe nodded but said nothing. He was as confused as Liehm was upset.

"But you're dead!" Liehm shouted hysterically, all his self-control gone now. "I saw Gregor shoot you!"

Chris shrugged and circled slowly around the room, maintaining his distance from Liehm till he was standing beside Joe. "Here I am," he said, spreading his arms. "Alive and kicking."

A wicked grin split the doctor's bruised face. "Not for long," he said, raising his gun.

Joe looked up at Chris, horrified. What was he doing?

Why was he offering Liehm such a perfect target?

Chapter

12

A SECOND LATER JOE had his answer.

A hand fell on Liehm's shoulder.

"Ah, Gregor," Liehm said excitedly, without turning. "See who I have found here? Now we can take care of all these Hardys at once."

"Sorry to disappoint you, Doctor."

Liehm turned. He barely had enough time to be surprised before a fist caught him hard on the chin, and he crumpled to the floor.

Frank stood over him, rubbing his knuckles. "That's for slugging me with that phone."

Chris picked up Liehm's fallen gun.

Joe clapped Frank on the back. "Nice work." He looked behind Frank. "Anybody else coming?"

Frank shook his head. "Just us—the two guards that came after us are downstairs, out of it."

"How'd you do it?"

"*He* did it." Frank nodded toward Chris. "He was planning to break in here and take on all of them single-handedly before I showed up. We triggered a few alarms, ambushed the guards that came . . ." Frank shrugged.

"You saved my life," Joe said to Chris.

"I'm the one who put it in danger in the first place," Chris said.

Joe grinned. "Nobody's responsible for what I do but me." He aimed an accusing finger at Chris. "But I still have a lot of questions for you!"

Chris smiled faintly and nodded. "I know I haven't been completely honest with you, but I'm ready to give you the answers you need."

"Good," Joe said.

"Hey!" Frank interrupted. "Where's Gregor?"

Joe's face dropped. "Gregor? He left after you set off the alarms the second time." He stared at Frank. "He didn't go past you?"

Frank shook his head.

"Then where *did* he go?" Chris asked.

"If you didn't pass him coming up from the service entrance, then he must have gone to the private staircase."

"I know where it is," Chris said. "Come on."

Frank and Joe followed him on a dead run back through the office till they came to a closed door. Chris tried the knob.

"He locked it behind him."

Joe tightened his lips in frustration. He thought of Gregor on the other side of the door. Then he pushed Chris aside. "Watch it."

Chris turned to him. "What are you doing?"

"I said, watch it."

Joe put his shoulder down and charged the door. The hinges groaned, and the wood around them cracked.

"Come on," Chris said, putting his hand on Joe's arm. "Let's go around the other way. That door's solid—it's not going to give."

"Give me Liehm's gun. I'll try shooting out the lock," Frank said, holding out his hand to Chris.

Joe pushed Frank's hand down. "One more time," he said. He charged the door again.

The wood split on one side. Joe kicked hard, and the door fell to the floor with a loud crash.

"Let's go," he said, stepping over it.

Behind the door was a short hallway leading to a set of stairs. Joe took the steps two at a time, expecting at any moment to find Gregor standing on one of the landings below him. But he reached the bottom of the staircase without an incident, Frank a step behind him.

Now another door stood in front of him. Without breaking step, Joe kicked it open—and found himself outside, looking into the parking garage.

The space where the Mercedes had been was empty.

"He got away." Joe shook his head and looked at Chris and Frank. "He's going to kill Janosik!"

"Kill him?" Frank grabbed his shoulders.

"Gregor and Liehm had some kind of fight," Joe said. "Gregor said Liehm could continue with his plan, but the only sure way to keep Janosik quiet was to kill him." He turned to Frank again. "And that's what he's going to do!"

"Easy," Frank said. "Lieutenant Considine is out at the hotel, with a lot of other cops. Nothing's going to happen to Janosik." He thought for a moment. "How did Liehm plan to keep Janosik from speaking?"

"I don't know," Joe said. "Liehm came to the hotel and showed Janosik something. Whatever it was really shook him. Wait a minute! It must've been that tape they said they were sending."

"And I bet I know where they're sending it," Frank said.

Joe nodded. "Jean Eykis. Has to be."

Frank turned. "Chris, what do you know about—"

But Chris wasn't there.

"He's got a real bad habit of disappearing," Joe said.

"I don't believe this!" Frank shook his head. "Come on, he must still be inside."

He and Joe raced back upstairs. At the entrance to the stairway, where Joe had knocked down the door, Frank stopped and picked something up off the floor.

"Liehm's gun," he said and frowned.

"What?" Joe asked.

"Why would he leave this?"

"I don't know!" Joe said angrily. "Nothing he's done so far has made any sense!"

Frank shook his head slowly. "I really thought Chris was going to level with us this time. Whose side is he on?"

"His own, apparently," Joe said.

Frank looked around the offices. "Liehm's gone!" he said. "We should have tied him up. How could we be so dumb? You know, this place has even more computer equipment than Chris's basement."

"That's obviously the link between Chris and Gregor and Liehm—but what's it all mean?"

"I don't know," Frank said. "If we could get a look at that tape they sent Eykis, that might help us."

Joe nodded, then slapped his forehead. "Whoa. Hold on a minute." He ducked into another room.

When he came out, he grinned at Frank. "Almost forgot my skateboard."

Eykis seemed surprised to see Frank again so soon. After he introduced Joe, he told her why they'd come.

"We think whatever they sent you is the key to this whole case we're working on," he said.

"It might be some kind of set-up, or a frame," Joe added.

She shook her head sadly. "I don't think so." She put her hands on her desk and stood up, leaning on her fingertips. "Well—you might as well watch it. You'll see it sometime soon."

She led them down the hall into a small room that was empty except for a desk with a TV set and VCR and a few chairs.

"This came about an hour ago," she said, unlocking the top drawer and taking out a videocassette. "The man who gave it to me asked me to call Liehm if I had any questions."

She inserted the cassette into the machine and turned back to them.

"Before I play this, I want you to know something. I've been writing for the *Tribune* for five years—and I've admired nobody in the world as much as I've admired Alexander Janosik." She sighed heavily. "This tape broke my heart."

Frank met her eyes and nodded but said nothing.

"That's the only reason I'm showing it to you—because I think it will break yours too. And because if there's any chance you can help prove it is a fake or a setup"—she managed a tired smile—"well, I'll take that chance. Otherwise, I'm stuck with a story that I really don't want to write."

She started the tape and sat down with them to watch.

It looked like the kind of film a bank's security camera would take, only with sound. The camera showed two men sitting at a table in an otherwise empty room. Frank didn't recognize either of them. Then Alexander Janosik entered.

Frank sat up and watched closely as the two men on screen rose to greet Janosik. They obviously knew one another, though their greetings were more courteous than friendly.

Janosik sat down at the table, facing the two men. They handed him a sheaf of notes and an envelope. Janosik glanced over the paper and opened the envelope.

It was full of hundred-dollar bills. Smiling at the two men, Janosik stood, shook hands again, and left the room.

The reporter stopped the tape.

"I assume you recognize Janosik—the two men you saw with him are Roger Douglas and David McCormick. They're both CIA."

Frank shook his head, unable to believe what he'd seen.

"Still think he's being framed?" Eykis asked bitterly. "Or are we the patsies in this picture?"

The Hardys said nothing. There was nothing they could say.

"Well, then, you'd better show yourselves out." Eykis stood and turned to go. "I have to get busy. I have a story to write."

* * *

Frank and Joe took the subway back to the Charles. Both were silent for most of the ride. Earlier that day, when he had listened to Janosik talk about what had happened to his country, Joe had thought of him as a patriot and hero. Now he didn't know what to think. How could he doubt the evidence of his own eyes?

"Frank," he asked. "Do you believe what we just saw?"

His brother took a long time answering. "I have to," he said finally. "But it doesn't make sense. Why would Janosik take a payoff? He doesn't seem like the kind of man who needs—or wants—a lot of money." He shook his head. "It just doesn't make sense."

"Nothing about this case makes sense," Joe agreed.

Frank knotted his hands together, frustrated. "I can't help the feeling that the clue we need is right in front of us, and we're just missing it. Maybe we ought to call in the police."

"The police? You mean Considine?" Joe asked, opening the door to their hotel room. "I don't think he wants to hear anything more from us."

He walked in the room and stopped suddenly.

"Oh, I wouldn't say that," a familiar voice said. "There's a whole lot more I want to hear from you. Only I'd rather not talk here."

The lights came on. Lieutenant Considine was

sitting on one of the beds. Two uniformed police officers stood by the window.

Considine motioned the two officers forward. "Let's take a little trip to headquarters, shall we?"

Chapter

13

"I DON'T KNOW WHAT kind of police force you have in Bayport," Considine said, pacing back and forth in front of the small table where the Hardys sat—where they'd been sitting for the past four hours. "But here we don't look kindly on kids who fake graduate student IDs and break into hotels. I could throw the book at both of you!"

Joe glared at the lieutenant but held his tongue.

"Lieutenant, did you check those names we gave you—Gregor Krc, Finn Liehm?" Frank asked, taking another sip of the coffee in front of him. He'd almost nodded off twice during Considine's interrogation.

"I'm not interested in fantastic conspiracy stories, or how the Czech secret police is invading Boston Common." Considine tossed their phony ID cards on the table. "Let's start with where you got these!"

"Look," Frank began. "I told you—what's important here is that this Gregor Krc is on the loose and he intends to kill Janosik. Lieutenant, that's what you ought to be focusing on—"

"Don't you tell me what my job is!" Considine roared, slamming his hand down on the table right in front of Frank. Coffee sloshed from the cup onto the table.

His partner laid a restraining hand on Considine's arm.

"I'm going to walk out of this room for five minutes," the lieutenant continued softly, stabbing a finger in Frank's face. "When I come back, you boys had better be ready to give me some answers." He stalked out of the room, slamming the door behind him.

"The lieutenant gets a little intense sometimes." His partner, a detective named Mitchell, pulled up a chair and sat in front of them. "But he's an all-right guy." He smiled at Frank and Joe.

"Maybe before he comes back, you could tell me a little bit more about why you checked into the Charles—in the room right next door to Janosik's."

The brothers exchanged a knowing glance. They knew this game too well, having pulled it a few times themselves—the good cop–bad cop routine.

"Like we said," Joe began, "we felt Janosik's life might be in danger. We knew that they—

Gregor and Liehm, that is—were going to try to frame him somehow, so—"

"Please," the detective said, holding up his hand. "No more talk about Janosik being framed—we've all seen the film on the local newscasts tonight."

Joe glowered at him. "That's not the point, is it? This guy Gregor was crazy enough to shoot at me—and now he's after Janosik! It doesn't matter whether or not he took money from the CIA; his life's in danger!"

"So *you* say." Mitchell stood and began pacing.

"What about the kid whose skateboard I borrowed?" Joe asked. "His name's on it. Why don't you call and ask him about the shooting at the hotel?"

The detective smiled faintly, as if to let Joe know he didn't believe that part of his story, either. "We'll try that in the morning. For now, I'd like to go back to where you got these IDs—"

"Hold it." Considine walked back into the room, madder than he'd been before. Joe braced himself for another round of questions.

"Let 'em go," Considine said flatly.

Joe swiveled around to stare first at Frank, then at Considine.

"Let us go?" Joe asked.

"Let them go?" Mitchell repeated.

"You heard me!" Considine roared. "Let them go! FBI says the guys they're talking about—

Gregor and Liehm—really are Czech agents. We've got orders to arrest them on sight. And those two guys we picked up unconscious at that Video Imaging place—they're STB, too.''

He turned to Frank and Joe. "You must have some heavy friends in Washington, because they told us to let you walk—no questions asked.''

Frank tried to hide a smile. "Friends in Washington" meant one thing to him: the Gray Man and the Network. Despite the trouble they often had working with America's most secret intelligence network, sometimes the connection proved useful.

"We'd be glad to stay and help you look for Liehm and Gregor, Lieutenant," Frank said. "We've seen them close up—"

"Their pictures will be coming over the wire. I think we can manage without your help." Considine motioned behind them through the open door, and a uniformed officer brought in two suitcases. "I took the liberty of having your bags packed and brought here." Considine looked at his watch. "The first plane leaves Logan at seven this morning. Catch it. And I don't want to see you guys playing detective in my town again, is that clear?''

Frank and Joe stood but said nothing.

Considine pulled the IDs the Beast had given them out of their wallets. "I'll keep these, if you don't mind—even if you're not involved in the phony ID ring, like Washington says. I'd like them as little souvenirs.''

His grin vanished. "Make sure these boys get on that plane," he told Mitchell. "And then come see me—we have to beef up security for Janosik." He stalked out of the room.

As Frank and Joe reached the airport, a newspaper truck was just pulling up. Frank watched bale after bale of newspapers hit the sidewalk. "Hold on a minute," he said. Setting his suitcase down, he walked over and studied the headlines. "Janosik Took Money from CIA," they screamed. Janosik's picture ran next to the article, a shot the paper must have had on file. He was speaking in front of a crowd somewhere, and the photographer had caught him in midsentence, his mouth open, his hand waving as he strove to make some point. He looked exactly as he had the day before in the park, when he'd been speaking of freedom and great men.

"It says he's speaking anyway." Mitchell read the article over Frank's shoulder. "You have to admire his guts."

Frank took a deep breath. "I do," he said. He turned away and picked up his suitcase again. "Come on—let's board."

"I don't like running away from a case like this, Frank," Joe grumbled.

"We're not running, Joe," Frank said. "The police know about Gregor and Liehm now, and you heard Considine say they're beefing up security for Janosik's speech. We've done everything we can. We do anything else, and Considine'll lock us up and throw away the key—never mind what our friend in Washington says."

Joe still wasn't convinced. "What about Chris?" he asked quietly.

Frank shook his head. "What about him? He's disappeared again—along with whatever proof he promised us of Janosik's innocence. If he wants to contact us, he knows where we are."

He was tired, he was disillusioned, and he was hungry—and all he wanted to do right then was sleep. "Wake me when we get to New York," he said, leaning back in his seat.

The Hardys took a cab to their house from the airport—and found a surprise waiting for them at home.

"Mom! Dad! You're home early!" Frank said as he walked into the living room.

"And so are you, from what Callie told us," Fenton Hardy said. "Fill me in on this Alexander Janosik case. I can't believe what the papers and TV stations are saying."

"It's even weirder than you've heard." Joe flopped down on the couch. He and Frank hadn't slept yet.

"Well?" their father asked.

Frank looked at Joe. "Chris?" Frank asked him.

Joe nodded. "Ask them."

"Chris?" Their mother looked puzzled. "Who's he?"

"*This* is Chris." Frank took out the driver's license he'd been carrying around and handed it to his mother. "Do you know him?"

She shook her head and passed it on to Fenton, who looked at it a little more closely.

"No, I don't know him," he said, reading the license. "Hardy? Is he related to us?"

"That's what we were going to ask you," Joe said.

Their parents stared at him. "Go ahead, we're listening."

Joe opened his mouth, then shut it. "You tell them," he said to Frank.

"He told us—" He stopped and tried to start again, unsure of how to ask the question without seeming ridiculous. He looked at Joe, who nodded vigorously, silently urging him on.

Frank decided there was no way to handle it without being ridiculous, so he just came out with it.

"He told us he's our older brother."

Frank and Laura Hardy stared at him, then Joe; then they turned to each other.

"Well?" Joe asked. "Is it true?"

His parents began to laugh.

"What kind of a question is that?" his father asked, shaking his head.

"Boys," his mother said, still trying to stop

112

laughing. "I can assure you you don't have an older brother! Whatever or whoever gave you that idea?"

"It has to do with this case," Frank said. He told them how he and Joe had met Chris down by the waterfront, how Chris had made his shocking claim, and how he'd known so much about their family.

"I saw his birth certificate—it's on file at City Hall. I also saw a school transcript."

"Frank," his father interrupted. "All those things can be faked. You ought to know that better than anyone else."

"But how could he get onto the City Hall computer system?"

"If you could, so could he," his father said firmly. "It interests me, though, that he knew so much about us. I think it's important we find out who this young man really is."

"We've been trying to do that," Joe said. "Only we haven't had much luck."

"There's something else about him, too," Frank said. "The videotape."

"Right," Joe said, grabbing his father by the arm. "Come watch this. If nothing else, at least you'll get a better look at him."

They all followed Joe into the den, where their Aunt Gertrude, who had returned from her visit, was sitting quietly, reading. She glanced up from her book. "What's all the fuss?"

"Just a little confusion, Aunt Gertrude," Joe said. "It has to do with our older brother."

"Oh." Aunt Gertrude began to read her book again. Then she frowned and looked up. "What did you say?"

Frank inserted the videotape and started it up. "He brought this with him when he came to meet us at the waterfront—said it would help prove Janosik was innocent."

They all settled down to watch the tape.

"What does it mean—'DD insertion'?" their father asked as the words appeared on the screen.

"We don't know," Frank said, shaking his head.

When they came to the close-up of the young soldier, Frank froze the tape, and turned to his parents.

"Does this help—does he look at all familiar?"

Both shook their heads.

"I don't understand." Aunt Gertrude spoke up from her chair in the corner. "Are you trying to identify that actor?"

"Actor?" Frank echoed.

"That's right, Frank." She shook her finger. "Don't you recognize this film?"

Frank shook his head. "Tell me."

She stood and walked to the screen. "This is a scene from *Deadly Deception*—that big suspense movie from a couple of years ago. This is the scene where they kill General Voroloff." She pointed at Chris's face and frowned. "This man's face doesn't look familiar. I was quite sure that another actor played this part. Oh, well,'' she said, sitting back down. ''I must have been wrong.''

''No, Aunt Gertrude,'' Frank said, as understanding dawned on him at last. ''No, you weren't wrong!'' He turned to Joe. ''Get it? DD insertion—''

''*Deadly Deception* insertion!'' Joe said excitedly. ''Somehow, Chris's face has been inserted on top of the original actor's!''

''Right.'' Frank nodded. ''So he never killed anybody.''

Joe balled his right hand into a fist and smacked it into his left palm. ''And that could mean Janosik never took that money, either! The whole thing's a fake!''

Chapter

14

"A FAKE?" LAURA HARDY ASKED. "How can you fake a film?"

"We're not talking about film, Mom," Frank said. "We're talking about videotape. It doesn't record pictures, it records data magnetically—like audio cassettes, or computer disks."

"So Chris used all those computers to help Krc and Liehm make this phony videotape?" Joe asked.

"Right," Frank said.

"I'm afraid I still don't understand," their mother said.

Frank sat down next to her. "There's a piece of equipment called a photo imager. It breaks up any photo into little dots—"

"Like on a TV set," his mother said.

"Exactly," Frank nodded. "Once you have an image broken and recorded, you can use a computer to move it around any way you want. It's

how they colorize old black-and-white movies."
He shook his head. "The company was called
Video Imaging," he said to himself. "I should
have seen it!"

"Easy, Frank." His father put a hand on his
shoulder. "What you're talking about doesn't
sound quite as simple as colorizing film. I didn't
know things like this were possible."

"They sure are, Dad," he said. "In a few years
this'll seem like kid stuff. The *Deadly Deception*
tape must have just been a test. Making the videotape of Janosik taking the bribe, that was the
real project."

He shook his head. "It must have taken them
months—maybe even a year. They probably began with a real tape of Janosik meeting those two
CIA guys—then changed it to smear him."

"And that must be where Chris came in. He
worked with them to develop that tape," Joe said.
"So his 'proof' of Janosik's innocence—"

"Was the tape that he brought with him, showing what kind of image manipulation was possible." Frank was still angry at himself. "I should
have seen it—they've been doing this kind of
thing on commercials for the last year or so."

"I'm starting to get lost," Fenton said. "I want
this whole story from the beginning. Come on."

Frank and Joe followed their father into his
study and laid out the whole story for him. When
his sons had finished talking, Fenton Hardy
stood. "This Chris sounds like a very mixed-up

young man," he said. "He can't seem to make up his mind whose side he's on."

Frank nodded. "Once he found out the tape he'd helped put together was going to the press and TV stations, he just took off, I guess."

"Sounds like you don't really believe that, Frank."

"I don't know, Dad." Frank smiled for a second. "I kind of liked the guy. And last night, I thought he was going to stick with us."

"He may surprise you yet," Fenton Hardy frowned as he concentrated. "Well, the first thing we have to do is get Janosik's name cleared."

"We can't just tell everyone the tape's a fake, though," Frank said. "It will take some proof—probably even beyond the phony *Deadly Deception* tape."

"From what you told me, I'd say the best place to get that proof is in Boston—at that place you broke into, Video Imaging," his father said.

Frank cleared his throat, glancing at Joe. "Uh, Dad, we're not supposed to go back there. We had a sort of run-in with a police lieutenant. . . ."

"You left that part out of your story." Fenton Hardy raised an eyebrow. "Never mind. One of the people I worked with on the force in New York is pretty important up there now. He should be able to smooth the way for us."

Joe and Frank exchanged sheepish grins.

Their father picked up the phone and dialed. "Yes, I'll hold." He picked up a pencil and started tapping it absentmindedly on his desk. "We'll take the next shuttle up."

"Right, Dad," said Joe. He turned to Frank, whispering, "I'd love to see the look on Considine's face when he sees us again."

Frank nodded, grinning.

"They're putting me through. We'll have this cleared up in a minute," their father said, leaning back in his chair. "Ah, yes—can you get me Ben Considine's office, please?"

Joe's mouth dropped open.

"Ben, Fenton Hardy here. . . . Yes, it has been a long time. I wonder if—"

As one, Joe and Frank got up quietly and headed for the door.

"Hold on a minute, Ben." Fenton covered the receiver. "What's the matter with you two? Don't you want to tell Lieutenant Considine what you've found out?" he asked.

They both shook their heads.

"We're kind of tired of talking to the police, dad." Frank smiled weakly. "You do it."

The plane ride to Boston was just long enough to be uncomfortable for Frank and Joe. They'd had to explain to their father why they hadn't been entirely truthful with Lieutenant Considine. By the time they reached Cambridge again, though, they had cleared that up.

Considine met them at the precinct house.

"Fenton!" he said. The two men shook hands. Then he stared at Frank and Joe.

"I knew that name was familiar," he said, scowling at them. Then he broke into a smile. "You kids remind me of myself, when I was younger—real troublemakers," he said, turning to Fenton Hardy. "Like when we were on the force in New York, Fenton, right?"

"Not quite," Fenton Hardy said. "We always worked with our superior officers—not against them." Frank and Joe knew those words were meant for them—a not-so-subtle reminder that if they wanted to be detectives, they had to learn to cooperate with the law.

Frank moved the subject to more comfortable territory. "I think the thing to do—with your help, Lieutenant," he added, "is to check out Video Imaging again. That's where we'll find proof of how they made these tapes."

"Yeah," Joe said. "We didn't exactly give it a thorough going-over before."

Fenton nodded. "Seems like a good idea to me. Can you spare a few men to help?"

Considine shook his head. "I haven't had a chance to check the place out at all—the new 'proof' about Janosik has the campus up in arms. Demonstrations are starting already—"

He frowned. "And we're still waiting for the FBI to get us pictures of those two—Krc and Liehm. With all the VIPs in town for Janosik's speech, I need everyone I have on campus."

Frank thought for a moment. "I know who could help us, Lieutenant. There's a student on campus who's a real computer expert."

"Get him down here," Considine said, glancing at his watch. He pointed Frank to an empty desk. "Use that phone." He turned to Fenton. "I'll count on you to keep everything under control. I've got to get back to the JFK Center."

Fenton nodded.

Frank called the Beast and explained why they needed his help.

"Wow," he said when they were finished. "They must really have some hardware to pull that trick. I'll be there in five minutes."

He was, and a few minutes later the four of them were in a borrowed police car on their way to downtown Cambridge. Fenton drove, with Joe in the front seat next to him and Frank and the Beast—who introduced himself as Larry—in back.

"Right here?" their father asked, pulling into the parking garage next door.

"This is it," Frank said.

"I never thought I'd see this place again." Joe shook his head, thinking of how close he'd come to dying in that building.

"I've been here before—only at night, though," the Beast said, getting out of the car. "We're going to Video Imaging—right?"

The three Hardys stared at him.

"My friend Chris works here," the Beast explained.

"Hold it," Frank said, pulling him back into the car. "Chris? Chris Hardy?"

"Nah," the Beast said. "Chris Bayer."

Fenton smacked the steering wheel. "Chris Bayer," he said. "Of course."

"You know him, Dad?"

"I did." He turned and faced his sons. "Chris is the son of a man I knew years back. Walter Bayer, a key witness in a mob case we were prosecuting in New York. His testimony helped put a big mob boss behind bars—"

"Tom Luther?" Joe asked. He remembered his father talking about the case a long time ago.

"Tom Luther." Fenton nodded. "His people killed Walter and his wife. Chris was about five or six at the time, but he'd seen the murder, so the mob was after him."

He shook his head. "When Laura and I heard about it, we took Chris in. It was only for half a year, and we had to keep it quiet. We were always afraid they'd track Chris down and kill him, too."

"No wonder you didn't recognize his picture," Joe said.

"It's been a long time," Fenton said. "Then the FBI decided he'd be safer if they moved him to another city, under the witness protection program." He took a deep breath. "It really shook your mother up when they took him away. Such a little boy being sent somewhere to new parents where he didn't know anyone.''

Frank dug Chris's license out of his pocket and showed it to the Beast. "Is this the guy?"

"That's him," the Beast said. He took the license from Frank and looked at it. "Excellent forgery—Chris really is much better at this than I am."

Frank took the license back. "What else can you tell us about him?"

The Beast frowned. "Not much. We used to meet here, or at his place."

"All the way out in Northampton?" Joe asked. "That's at least a two-hour drive from here."

"Northampton?" the Beast shook his head. "No, his apartment's here in Cambridge, right on Windham Street."

"It might be worth taking a look at that apartment, Dad," Frank said.

Fenton Hardy nodded, starting up the car again. "Let's try there first."

They found Windham easily enough. Except for the motel on the corner, it was a street of quiet frame houses. The one they pulled up at had been a bright yellow. Now it needed a fresh coat of paint.

"This is it," the Beast said.

"Looks like student housing to me," Fenton Hardy said.

Larry nodded. "Most of the block is. Chris has

been here for a while, though. He's really got the basement fixed up."

"Let's check it out," Joe said.

They went down a short flight of steps to a separate basement entrance, with its own bell. They rang it.

No answer.

Frank wasn't too surprised. He hadn't expected it to be this easy to find Chris—not after the wild goose chase he'd led them on.

"Dad! Frank! Come here!"

Joe knelt at one of the basement windows. "There's somebody in there, but he's not moving!"

Fenton Hardy gently pushed his son aside. "Let me see, Joe." Frank peered over his father's shoulder. "Dad, it looks like Chris!"

Fenton nodded. "Let's get in there." He took off his jacket, wrapped it around his fist, then smashed the window. Joe reached through the broken glass, unlatched the window, climbed inside, and gasped.

"What's that smell?"

"Gas." Fenton was right behind his son. "Don't touch a light switch, or do anything to cause a spark. You could turn the whole place into an inferno. Let's get Chris and get out of here."

He turned to the Beast, who peered nervously through the window. "Larry, ring doorbells—get anybody who's in the house out on the street."

The Beast left. Fenton and Joe moved forward.

Chris lay sprawled in the middle of the living room floor. Joe knelt down, feeling for a pulse. "He's not dead, just unconscious. And he has a very nasty lump on the head."

"All right," Fenton said. He glanced around. "Let's pick him up—and get out of here."

"Dad, wait!" Joe had caught sight of something around the corner, in the next room.

He stepped back and found himself in the kitchen. The oven door was open, and on the floor lay another body, that of a woman.

Joe bent down to look closer. Then he heard a noise behind him.

Ludvik—the man who'd posed as the elevator operator the night before at Video Imaging—was tapping on the back window. He smiled when he saw he'd gotten Joe's attention.

"What the—" Joe began.

Then he saw the cigarette lighter in Ludvik's right hand. The STB man flicked it, sending a small flame shooting up into the air.

Still smiling, he kicked in the window, tossing the lighter into the kitchen.

Joe threw his hands over his face.

But that didn't stop the explosion that followed.

Chapter

15

FRANK SAW JOE HURTLING toward him—then a ball of hot air slammed him against the wall.

A split second later the entire room erupted into fire.

He struggled to his feet.

Joe was sprawled against one wall.

Fenton Hardy lay on the floor, pinned under a huge bookcase that had toppled over. Chris had been thrown clear. Flames were already licking at the bookcase.

Joe's eyes flickered open, and he began to cough. "Frank, what—"

"Help me!" Frank cried. "We've got to get this bookcase off Dad!"

Joe staggered to his feet.

"Mr. Hardy! Frank! Joe!" The Beast was at the window. "Are you all right?"

"Larry—get in here! We need your help!" Frank yelled. He knelt beside his father. Fenton

Hardy's eyes were shut, and blood trickled from a small gash on his forehead.

Larry climbed gingerly in through the window.

"Come on, come on," Frank called impatiently. The room was already starting to fill with smoke.

Joe and the Beast knelt beside him.

"Don't try to pick this thing up," Frank said. "Let's just lift it a little, and roll him out from under it. Together—one, two, three, lift!"

The bookcase didn't move.

"Too heavy," the Beast said, coughing. It was getting hard to breathe in the room.

"Take some of these books out!" Frank frantically began scooping books from the shelves and throwing them to the side.

"Again!" Frank yelled. They lifted the bookcase up a few inches.

Frank rolled his father out from underneath.

"Joe—take Chris." Frank's voice was raw as he picked up his father, slinging him over his shoulder. He opened the front door and staggered out onto the front lawn.

Fenton Hardy began coughing.

"Easy, Dad," Frank said. "You'll be all right." A group of students who must have been in the other apartments in the building crowded around.

"Don't just stand there!" Frank yelled. "Get the fire department!"

"Frank!" Joe and the Beast came out of the

apartment, carrying Chris. They lay him on the ground next to Fenton Hardy. Joe collapsed to his knees, gasping for breath. "Frank, there's a woman in the kitchen, unconscious!"

Frank glanced back at Chris's apartment. Smoke was billowing out through the front window.

Frank stood. "Keep the crowd back—I'm going in after her."

"Be careful!" Joe called out, struggling to his feet.

Frank nodded, bent low, and went in the front door.

He could barely see two feet ahead of him now—the fire was everywhere. He dropped to the floor to avoid the smoke and began slithering on his stomach in the direction of the kitchen.

How could the woman have survived? he asked himself.

And who was she, anyway?

Pushing that question to the back of his mind—there'd be time enough to answer it later, assuming there was a later—he moved forward. The heat grew more intense. He expected at any moment to feel the hot flames actually singe his hand.

Then he touched something so unexpected that he almost jumped to his feet.

Water!

He squinted and peered into the smoke.

The explosion had ripped some water pipes

loose. Water was spraying everywere around the kitchen, and a small shower of it had formed a puddle around—Jean Eykis!

He pulled her to him, and turned back toward the front door.

"What's taking him so long?" Joe asked, sitting on the front lawn beside his father. Chris had yet to stir, but his father had come around a few seconds ago and immediatcly started coughing. Larry had run off to look for some water for him.

"Shouldn't have let him go in there, Joe," his father said.

"Could you have stopped him, Dad?" Joe asked. "You know how hard it is to get Frank to change his mind once he's got it set on something." Joe spoke lightly, but he was worried. Frank had been gone almost a minute. The whole house was on fire now, flames and smoke billowing out of every window.

"I'm going in there after him, Dad," Joe said.

"No, wait," his father said, holding up his hand. They heard sirens in the distance, and a few seconds later a fire engine roared to a stop in front of the house.

"About time," Joe said. "Come on!" he yelled, rushing up to the firemen. "My brother's still in there!"

"All right," one said. He waved to the men behind him. "Let's go!"

Suddenly there was a huge roar behind them, like a clap of thunder. Joe turned. The building shuddered and leaned to one side.

"The crossbeams are giving way!" the fireman in charge shouted. The house shuddered again and collapsed forward. "Everybody back!"

"Frank!" Joe yelled and started toward the house.

"Easy, kid," the fireman grabbed his shoulder. "Nobody could have survived that."

"No!" Joe shouted, struggling free of the fireman's grasp. "Let me go!"

He shoved the fireman aside and moved forward.

"I appreciate the thought, but there's no one in there to save, Joe."

He turned. Frank stood behind him, holding Eykis in his arms.

"We had to go out the back," Frank said. "The flames cut us off." He smiled. "It's nice to know you care, though."

"It's not just that," Joe replied, trying hard not to let his relief show through. "You still owe me for the pizza."

"I thought you were headed for Video Imaging," Considine said, handing Fenton Hardy a bandage. The lieutenant had come as soon as he'd heard the report of the fire—and who was involved—over his radio.

"We were," Fenton said, wrapping it around his hand. "But something else came up." He filled Considine in.

"So now we've got to look out for this Ludvik guy, too," he said. He turned back to Frank and Joe. They were sitting on the street curb beside Chris, who had finally come around. An ambulance crew had arrived and had passed out bandages and oxygen to those who had been in the fire. They were still attending to Eykis—but it looked as if she was going to be all right, too.

"How's your friend, boys?"

"I'm all right, Lieutenant," Chris said.

"He's been filling in some of the missing pieces to the story," Frank explained.

"Last night at Video Imaging," Chris continued. "I started to follow you down the stairs—then someone smashed something over my head. The next thing I knew, I was in my own apartment with Gregor bending over me."

Frank smiled. "I knew you didn't run out on us."

Their father came and stood over the three of them.

"Hello, Chris," he said.

"Hello, Mr. Hardy," Chris replied. "It's been a long time."

Fenton nodded.

"I guess I've made an awful mess of things,

haven't I?'' Chris stared at the street in front of him.

"Nothing we can't fix, I hope," Fenton replied. "But how did you get mixed up with Krc and Liehm in the first place?"

"They came to me," Chris said, finally raising his gaze to meet Fenton Hardy's. "You see, I was doing some—things—for some friends of mine at school." He glanced over quickly at the Beast, who glanced quickly at Frank and Joe.

"The phony ID ring," Considine grumbled. "I'll want to talk to you some more about this, young man. You have a lot of people on campus very upset. I hear there may be someone else involved in this as well, Larry," he said to the Beast.

Larry gulped.

Chris continued his story. "Liehm heard about what I was doing with the imager, I guess, and came to me to help him with this project he was starting. It was an incredible opportunity, they had a lot of money backing them up. I worked for almost a year with that crazy spy film—"

"Deadly Deception," Joe said.

"Right, and when that came out so well, Liehm said they were going to do something else using the techniques I'd developed, and if I didn't help they'd turn me in to the police for the phony ID stuff I'd done!"

"What made you decide to stop them?" Frank asked.

"Seeing Janosik speak," Chris said. "I know it sounds corny, but—"

Joe smiled. "It doesn't sound corny at all."

"Why were you pretending to be our brother?" Frank asked.

Chris shrugged. "That's an ID I've been using for a while. I did up the driver's license, the City Hall documents to show how much could be done. I guess I'd always had a secret wish that"—he looked up at Fenton Hardy—"well, that . . ."

"I understand," Fenton said, laying a hand on his shoulder.

"But why'd you run away that first night?" Frank asked.

"Because I didn't want to see you get killed! Your parents . . ." He swallowed. "The time I spent with them—I just couldn't bear to be responsible if anything happened to you, for what it would have done to them." He smiled weakly. "So that's it—the whole story."

"All right, Chris," Fenton said. "You'd better rest now." He turned to Considine. "Where's Janosik now?"

"He's speaking with a group of reporters—just the local press and TV people."

"Wait a minute," Frank said. "Jean Eykis is with the *Tribune*."

"Yeah, that's right," Considine said. "Gene Eykis. I checked his credentials myself before we allowed him to enter the room with Janosik."

"No," Frank said, a sudden chill running down his back. "You don't understand."

He pointed at the woman who lay unconscious on the stretcher.

"*That's* Jean Eykis!"

Chapter

16

CONSIDINE STARED FOR A MOMENT.

"Then who's with—oh, no." His eyes widened.

"Oh, yes," Frank said. "Gregor. It has to be." He described the man.

"That's him," Considine agreed. "But how could—"

Joe jerked a thumb at Chris. Considine snapped his fingers.

"That's why he brought me here," Chris realized. "He must have used the equipment in my other apartment to fake her press card."

"And that's why she was here," Frank said. "So she'd be out of the way." He looked up at Considine. "He means to kill Janosik, Lieutenant."

Considine got on the police radio. "Get me Mitchell—he's at the JFK Center symposium. And I mean now!"

He turned back to the Hardys. "All of you—Chris, Frank, Joe, that includes you—get in my car. I'll want you there to help us identify him and the other men."

The three nodded and hopped in the back seat. Their father got in the front on the passenger side. Larry was sent home in a squad car.

"Mitchell, this is Considine. Don't talk, just listen. Stay close to Janosik—got that? One of the reporters there is the guy we want. He's going by the name Gene Eykis. I'll be there in five minutes."

He replaced the handset and climbed in the front seat.

"Fasten your seat belts, boys," he said, switching on the siren. Considine slammed the car into gear, leaving behind the firemen to fight the still-smoldering blaze.

When they arrived, the JFK Center was chaos. Demonstrators surrounded the entire complex, brought there by the news that Janosik was a CIA plant.

"If only they knew the truth," Joe said as they pulled up across the street.

"They'll find out soon enough," Considine said, getting out of the car. "That isn't going to help us right now, unfortunately. We're going to have to go through them to get to Janosik."

He forced a path through the demonstrators—and they followed in his wake. Frank hoped the walls of the lecture hall inside were thick enough so that Janosik couldn't hear what the demonstrators were saying about him.

Finally, they reached the door to the library-lecture hall complex. A guard waved them in, holding back the fringes of the crowd. "They're in the reception hall upstairs. Second door on your left, Lieutenant."

"Thanks, Johnson." Considine clapped the man on the shoulder and led them up the stairs. Inside the hall they found Janosik mingling with reporters and other members of the symposium. Considine's partner Mitchell stood quietly at his side. There was a small podium set up at the far end of the room, where Janosik would take questions from the press later.

"I don't see Krc," Considine said, frowning. "Are any of the others here?"

Frank looked the room over. It was almost as crowded in there as it had been outside. He shook his head, as did Joe and Chris.

"No sign of them, Lieutenant," Frank said, speaking for all three of them.

"Stick close to Janosik, then." He motioned to Fenton Hardy, and the two of them went off to check the hall.

Janosik smiled when he caught sight of the Hardys.

"Frank and Joe," he said, shaking hands with each of them enthusiastically. "I'm very glad to see you again."

"And we're glad to see you, too, sir," Frank put in.

Just then the catcalls of the demonstrators outside got very loud. They were saying some very cruel things about Alexander Janosik.

"Free speech," Janosik said ruefully, trying to make light of the moment. "It is a wonderful thing to see in action—no matter what the cause."

"We know you haven't done anything wrong, sir," Frank began. Joe nodded his agreement. "That's partially why we're here."

Janosik's eyes glistened. "I am glad you believe me." He frowned. "This tape—Liehm showed it to me. I do not understand how he did it, but it is preposterous! Never would I take money from the CIA."

Chris spoke up for the first time. "I'm afraid that it's my fault you're in all this trouble."

"Oh?" Janosik raised an eyebrow. "And who are you?"

"This is Chris Bayer, Mr. Janosik," Frank said.

Janosik bowed his head slightly. "I am pleased to meet you, Mr. Bayer."

Chris explained what he had done. When he was through, Janosik shook his head gently. "That is not your fault, Chris." He smiled. "You were weak, when you perhaps should have been strong, but to say this is your fault is nonsense. I know whose fault this is."

A bearded man motioned to Janosik.

"I believe it is time for me to talk to the press," Janosik said, nodding in the direction of the podium. "You'll excuse me."

He strode off, but before he could reach his place at the podium, Considine reentered the room and pulled him aside to whisper a few words in his ear. Janosik nodded. Considine walked behind the lectern and began to speak.

"I'm Lieutenant Ben Considine of the Cambridge Police Force," he began. "If I could just have your attention for a moment—"

The crowd gathered in a semicircle facing the podium. The press, Frank could see, shoved closer to the front. I guess they have a lot of questions for Janosik, Frank thought. He could hardly blame them.

"We've all seen the stories in this morning's papers," Considine continued, "and on TV. Some of you have even written them." The audience gave a few appreciative snickers.

Considine leaned forward at the lectern. "I want you all to know that based on information we have recently uncovered, I can tell you that these stories—and the videotape they are based on—are absolute lies. Alexander Janosik is not now, nor has he ever been, an agent of our government." He smiled. "Though we're very glad to have him in this country."

Considine held out his hand. "Mr. Janosik,"

he said calmly, indicating the lectern. "The stage is yours."

Janosik smiled and moved forward.

The room erupted into bedlam.

Frank exchanged a knowing glance with his brother. He began to think things were going to work out after all.

Just then Frank saw Gregor enter the room and reach into his jacket pocket while heading for Janosik.

"Joe!" Frank said. His brother turned, and at that instant Gregor caught sight of them as well. He cursed and disappeared into the hallway.

"Let's go! Chris, stay with Janosik!" He and Frank began moving as fast as they could through the crowd. They reached the hallway. Gregor was nowhere in sight.

"This way!" Joe said, pointing off to his right, back toward the staircase they had come up.

With Frank a step behind, Joe leapt down the stairs, taking them two at a time. This time, he swore, Gregor wasn't going to get away. He'd chase him down on foot if he had to.

They bounded past the guard at the entrance and out into the crowd of demonstrators.

"There he is! And Liehm's with him!" Joe yelled. He pointed down a path that led into JFK Park, the same path they'd taken with Janosik the day before. Gregor and Liehm were on that path, running past the pillars engraved with the late president's speeches.

The STB agents cut across the park diagonally, heading for the far corner near the river. Frank and Joe set off in pursuit, steadily closing the gap.

A few hundred feet in front of them, the park ended at an intersection where two busy roads crossed, one running parallel to the river, the other back over it into downtown Boston.

Gregor and Liehm reached the intersection and started through it. A car screeched to a halt, barely missing them. As they got to the other side, another car plowed into the one that had stopped. In seconds the entire intersection was jammed with cars. Drivers began honking their horns and screaming at one another.

"Great." Joe stopped at the corner, breathing heavily. "How are we going to get across that—"

Frank never missed a step. He scrambled onto the hood of one car, and jumped from that one onto the hood of the next, leap-frogging his way across the intersection. Joe followed him. They left behind many angry drivers.

Directly across the intersection, an old brick building, covered with ivy, stood on the river's edge—one of the many boathouses that dotted the banks of the Charles. There was a small motorboat tied to the dock at the back of it. Gregor and Liehm had apparently seen it, too, for they were already splashing through the water toward it.

Joe waded in after them, the shock of the cold river water sending chills up his back.

"Hey, what are you doing? You can't take that boat!" Two students stood on the sloping wooden launch platform next to the dock, about to launch a two-man scull. One of them gestured angrily at Gregor. "That's not—"

The STB man raised a gun.

The student backed off, dropping his oars. His friend did likewise. Both turned and ran, disappearing around the far side of the boathouse.

Gregor and Liehm clambered into the boat. Liehm started the engine.

"Oh, no!" Joe yelled, watching the motorboat pull out onto the river. "They're getting away!"

Chapter

17

"MAYBE NOT," FRANK SAID. He picked up the scull the students had set down and dragged it to the water. "Come on!"

Joe shook his head. "Are you crazy? We'll never catch them in that!"

"At least we can keep them in sight," Frank said. Joe shrugged and picked up a single set of oars. Frank settled himself in the back of the boat, and Joe took the front.

Slowly at first, then picking up speed as they synchronized their rowing motion, they moved out on the river.

But their best speed was nowhere near fast enough. The motorboat was rapidly pulling away.

"They won't get far!" one of the students who had dropped the small scull shouted from the dock. "The gas tank's almost empty!"

Sure enough, up ahead on the river the motorboat had slowed, and as they watched, stopped.

Frank and Joe resumed their own efforts with redoubled speed, and rapidly closed on them.

Gregor raised his gun when he saw them coming. Taking careful aim, he squeezed off a shot.

The bullet buried itself in the hull of the Hardys' boat.

Their scull shot past the stopped STB men. Joe raised his oar and swung it, knocking the gun out of Gregor's hands. It went spinning into the river.

Liehm sat motionless in the small motorboat, holding another gun on his lap.

"What are you waiting for, fool?" Gregor shouted. "Shoot them! Shoot!"

"No, Gregor." Liehm dropped his gun into the bottom of the boat. He raised his hands. "The time for running, for fighting, is over."

With an inarticulate cry, Gregor bent over and snatched the gun Liehm had dropped. Joe leapt across the water into the motorboat and onto Gregor. As the two wrestled for control of the gun, they pitched into the water.

Wading into the water had been a bracing shock, but diving in was as if a cold fist had suddenly clenched tight around his heart, driving the breath from his body. Joe surfaced, gasping for air.

Gregor was swimming for shore.

Thrusting aside any exhaustion he felt, Joe set out after him.

He'd sworn it—this time Gregor wasn't getting away.

Behind him, Frank struggled to get the scull moving again with one oar. Joe heard him yelling something, but it didn't matter.

He had to catch Gregor.

He reached the riverbank and dragged himself onto the shore. Gregor was barely fifty feet ahead of him.

He put on a burst of speed. Gregor turned and saw him coming. There was a hint of fear in the man's eyes.

At that instant Joe knew he was going to catch him.

Gregor stopped running halfway up the hill between the JFK Center and the Hotel Charles, right beside the construction pit. He turned to face Joe.

"Hardy," he said, breathing heavily. Joe approached to within ten feet of him and stopped. "You have been a source of great annoyance to me."

"My pleasure," Joe said.

Gregor shook his head. "Still you make jokes. Good." He reached down and pulled a knife out of his boot. "You will die laughing then."

He moved forward, brandishing the knife like an expert. Joe stepped back quickly, his eyes tracking Gregor's wrist. If his concentration slipped for even a second, the knife would be in him.

"No jokes now, eh?" Gregor taunted, circling him.

"What kind would you like to hear?" Joe asked warily.

Gregor lunged forward. At the last possible second, Joe dodged. As Gregor passed him, he pushed the STB man into the wooden fence around the construction pit. With a loud crack, the flimsy wood gave way. Gregor went tumbling down into the construction area itself.

Joe jumped down after him, tumbling head-over-heels. He came to a stop and scrambled to his feet.

A two-by-four missed his head by inches.

Gregor must have lost his knife when he fell into the pit, but he'd found something to replace it quickly enough. Building materials littered the floor of the pit—many of them lethal looking. Gregor had wasted no time in choosing another weapon.

The STB man laughed and swung the beam around again. This time it caught Joe full in the chest, and he was slammed to the ground. He lay there stunned, unable for a moment to breathe, or even to think.

"Hah!" Gregor hovered over him, raising his improvised club high over his head, his face twisted with anger and pleasure.

"Now, Hardy, I am rid of you forever!"

He brought the beam crashing down.

Chapter

18

JOE ROLLED TO HIS SIDE. The beam missed him by inches, raising a cloud of dust as it smashed into the ground. Gregor raised it again and brought it down—and again Joe rolled out of harm's way.

This time, as he rolled over, Joe snatched up a handful of dirt and flung it in Gregor's eyes.

"Arrgh!" Blinded, Gregor staggered backward. Joe scrambled to his feet and kicked out, knocking the beam from the agent's hand. He followed through with a right to the jaw that sent the STB man stumbling into a pile of cinder blocks.

Gregor wiped dirt from his eyes. He grabbed a cinder block off the pile next to him, hurling it at Joe, who barely managed to dodge.

"Don't play caveman!" Joe taunted him. "Show me some secret agent tricks!"

Gregor snarled and picked up another cinder block. He threw this one even harder.

Joe stepped quickly to his right. The block whistled by and grazed him lightly on the side of the leg.

He fell to the ground as if he'd been shot.

With an awful smile, Gregor picked up another cinder block and moved toward him.

Joe scrambled backward—until he felt something hard at his back.

A cement wall. The foundation of the building being built there. He dragged himself to his feet.

"You can't run any more, Hardy," Gregor said. "Now—"

Springing off the wall, Joe shot forward to drop-kick Gregor in the stomach with both feet. Gregor grunted heavily and dropped the cinder block.

"It is not over yet, Hardy," Gregor said, swaying on his feet, his breath coming in harsh, ragged gulps.

"Isn't it?" Joe asked, wiping the dirt off his face. "Janosik's safe—and you're dead on your feet."

"Not yet," Gregor said. With the last of his strength, he half swung, half fell at Joe. Joe dodged the blow.

Now it was his turn. He balled his right hand into a fist and swung with all his might.

His knuckles connected with Gregor's jaw with

a satisfying *crack*—and Gregor toppled to the ground like a fallen tree.

Joe stood over him, breathing heavily. He was covered with dirt. His jacket was torn, and his body ached all over, but he felt pretty good.

"Joe!" He turned. Frank was standing above him, looking down into the construction pit.

"Everything all right down there?" his brother called down.

"Under control," Joe called back.

"You could have waited for me, you know," Frank said accusingly.

"Oh, no," Joe replied, rubbing his hand and staring down at Gregor. "This one was all mine."

"We caught Ludvik at the airport. He'll be sharing that cell with Gregor and Liehm—for a long, long time," Considine said. "In this country. Prague has officially denied any connection with Liehm's project, and any of the people we've taken into custody."

"I find that hard to believe," Frank said. He and Joe, in dry clothes they'd borrowed from one of the Beast's dorm neighbors, sat at a table back in the Cambridge precinct house, their father and Considine across from them.

"So do I," Considine said. "But we're not going to complain. By the way," he added, "we finally turned up that kid you borrowed the skateboard from. He'll be testifying about Krc attacking you from his car. He also asked if the 'government agent' was done with his board.''

Joe laughed. "Well, I guess you can tell us where to return it.''

A uniformed officer opened the door. "Excuse me, Lieutenant, those two young men you wanted to see are here.''

Considine nodded. "Show them in.''

The officer stepped aside, and Chris and Larry walked into the room. They sat down nervously next to Frank.

Fenton Hardy smiled. "Now, Ben, what we were talking about before—''

"Yes,'' Considine had a grim stare for the newcomers. Both shifted in their seats, looking uncomfortable. "I've talked with the authorities here at Harvard, and based on both your records, and the good words of Mr. Hardy here''—he nodded at Fenton—"the university people and the district attorney's office are willing to drop all charges against you two. Under one condition.''

Chris looked up unbelievingly. "Name it.''

The Beast nodded his assent.

Considine smiled. "You are both directed to report to the superintendent of continuing education, for teaching assignments in computer education. You'll each be required to teach five hundred hours of classes.''

Larry gulped. "I've never been very good at communicating with other people.''

"Well, here's your chance to learn,'' Considine

said. "Their equipment may not be as fancy as what you're used to—"

"I know where they can get more—if they want it," Chris said. "A whole basement full."

Considine nodded. "I'm sure they'd be delighted to accept."

Frank and Joe exchanged smiles.

The door to the room opened again, and Alexander Janosik walked in.

"Mr. Janosik!" Joe exclaimed, standing. "What brings you here?"

The old man was wearing a Harvard sweatshirt that made him look like a grandfatherly undergraduate. "I came to thank you all for everything, and to ask you to attend my closing speech tomorrow at the symposium."

"We really should be getting back home," Fenton Hardy said regretfully, looking at his watch.

"Dad," Joe pleaded. "Can't we stay and hear the speech?"

"Well, wrapping this case up is a good excuse for a celebration, isn't it?" Fenton smiled. "All right, we'll stay in Cambridge tonight."

"Now you're talking. I'll even treat you and the boys to dinner," Considine said.

"No, no." Fenton shook his head. "My treat."

"Maybe Mr. Janosik would like to join us, too," Frank suggested.

Janosik bowed. "I would be honored."

Fenton smiled at his sons. "I'll call your mother and tell her not to expect us home." He turned to Chris. "And there's something else I'd like to tell her about, too."

"Where should we eat?" Frank asked.

"I know this pizza joint right around the corner," Chris suggested.

"I think something a little nicer," Fenton said. "Maybe an Italian restaurant, or—"

"Hamburgers!" Janosik proudly proclaimed. "Very American. Especially with the cheese and bacon—excellent."

Joe clapped him on the back.

"How about it, Frank?" Chris asked. "Bacon cheeseburgers all right with you?"

"Frank likes his burgers plain—don't you, Frank?" Joe teased.

Frank shook his head, knowing when he was beaten. "Bacon cheeseburgers sound fine."

Frank and Joe's next case:

The Hardy brothers race to Seattle to help their father, Fenton, who stands accused of murder! In their father's rented house, they're met by burglars, who try to gun them down. When Frank and Joe follow their trail, they learn that valuable timber is being destroyed by a deadly virus. They also find that an entire town has been sealed off to prevent a mysterious epidemic.

Meanwhile Fenton Hardy is the hostage of a sinister scientist with a formula for certain death. And if the brother detectives can't reach him in time, he'll become the victim in a doomsday experiment in . . . *Disaster for Hire,* Case #23 in the Hardy Boys Casefiles™.